The Summer at Lyme

Laurence Fleming's first novel, *A Diet of Crumbs*, was published in 1959 by the Artemis Press, selected from a competition judged by a panel that included Nancy Mitford and Angus Wilson. At Cambridge he wrote scripts for the Footlights. He is co-author, with Alan Gore, of the bestselling *The English Garden* and, with Ann Gore and Clay Perry, of *Old English Villages*. He is author of *The One Hour Garden*, which he illustrated himself; of *Roberto Burle Marx, A Portrait* and of *On Torquemada's Sofa*. He has compiled two volumes of memories from British India under the title of *Last Children of the Raj*. He lives in St Leonard's-on-Sea, East Sussex.

The Summer at Lyme

Laurence Fleming

dexter
haven
PUBLISHING

Published in 2010 by Dexter Haven Ltd
Curtain House
134–146 Curtain Road
London EC2A 3AR

ISBN 978-1-903660-08-9

Front cover image courtesy of the National Portrait Gallery, *Sir
William Edward Parry* by Samuel Drummond; all other images
© Ken Leeder, with thanks to the Geffrye Museum.

Typeset by Dexter Haven Associates Ltd, London
Printed in Great Britain by CPI Cox & Wyman, Reading RG1 8EX

To Leslie and James

The reader is asked to imagine that all the novels of Jane Austen began at the same time, the summer of 1814.

I

1823

Elizabeth had asked that the doctor be brought to her, in her own sitting-room, as soon as he had finished his examination of her children.

It was not a large room, on the first floor facing the south-west, and it was particularly pleasant on very warm mornings in the summer. This morning, a very warm one indeed, it was filled with the scent of pinks and stocks and early roses. They stood, as nosegays, in jugs and vases on two of the tables and on her own desk.

She awaited the doctor quite calmly, not afraid of what he would say. In the last four weeks, all the children had gone down, one by one, with scarlet fever. The source of the infection was still not certain, but it was known to be present in the village, three miles away. At least she could now congratulate herself that, with all her precautions, no one else in the house had contracted it.

The younger servant girls, the most at risk, had all been sent home. The grooms and gardeners had been forbidden the house. Neighbours and visitors kept their distance; her husband and his steward conducted their business in the open air.

Elizabeth had undertaken the nursing herself, albeit with the devoted help of the children's nurse and the two nursery-maids. Soups, panadas, coddled eggs, jellies and creams, anything that was easy to swallow, had been produced in the kitchens with every care, and without complaint. Fortunately the month had been May, a peculiarly mild and dry one, and they had been able to keep the windows open all day long.

She had never had more than one moment's anxiety, were she to be honest with herself, in the whole four weeks; and that was when Alexander, aged two-and-a-half, was discovered fallen out of bed, with one side of his face a mass of bruises. But she hardly recognised the three little waifs who now inhabited the nursery, so badly had they all been pulled down.

Her attendance had been constant, being with them entirely during the day, sometimes sitting up with them all night, feeding them, reading to them, haunted always by the thought of what *might* happen rather than finding satisfaction in the fact that it had *not*. Her own health had suffered, very slightly.

The doctor did not keep her waiting long. Announced by the butler, he came smiling into the room, speaking as he entered.

"I can only say to you, Madam, that I bring you glad tidings of great joy. I have examined them with every skill at my disposal and can confidently say that there is no sign of any permanent damage."

Elizabeth offered him her hand.

"I am *very* glad to hear you say so. And, on my side, I must congratulate *you*—on the soundness of your advice and, indeed, the excellence of your remedies."

The doctor bowed.

"I believe the constancy of the nursing may also be quite justly praised," he said. "It is not often that I find my instructions so carefully followed—in general, in fact, I think I may say with confidence, they are scarcely followed at all—and in this happy result I believe the credit may be fairly divided between the doctor and the nurses."

Elizabeth smiled.

"We were more than happy, I can assure you, to follow those instructions, particularly as the results were to be seen so soon. While I cannot entirely attribute my children's recovery to their diet of goat's milk, I do believe it helped it very much."

The doctor smiled back.

"Do you mean to keep your herd of goats, now that the emergency is passed?"

"Most certainly I do. Mrs Reynolds has found an old receipt for the making of an excellent cream cheese—so rich and delicate that I sometimes wonder if we shall ever want to eat anything else."

"Then I am quite satisfied. At the same time, I am obliged to say that my *opinion* is that a complete change of air is now advisable. No one could quarrel with the quality of the air at Pemberley, but I think that benefit will be given by a complete change. In short, Madam, I must advise that you take your children to the sea."

"To the sea! But, my dear doctor, where are we to find lodgings at Scarborough or Bridlington, so late as we are in the season?"

"I cannot advise either. The air on that coast is altogether too harsh and only the healthy can benefit from it."

"Because everything nourishes what is strong already?"

"Yes, without doubt. Were your circumstances otherwise than as they are, I could not say this; but I think you must travel to the *south* coast."

Elizabeth sat down and motioned to the doctor to do the same.

"The south coast must be quite three hundred miles from here," she said. "Even supposing we could find somewhere to stay there—and this is already the third day of June—how would my poor patients fare upon the journey?"

"Your poor patients, Madam," said the doctor, spreading the tails of his coat as he sat down on a sofa, "have inherited an excellent constitution—from both their parents, as I judge. Certainly the journey will be long and slow but, with all the care they will receive, I cannot anticipate any danger; and the benefit, I can assure you, will be enormous."

After a moment, Elizabeth said: "I have a sister at Torbay, I suppose. Certainly she praises everything there and says she is as happy and as healthy as she ever expects to be."

"I am not acquainted with Torbay," remarked the doctor. "Indeed, I have never visited the south coast at all, and we may be quite sure that there are, by now, no rooms at Brighton, or indeed at Weymouth. But a certain patient that I have in Buxton, a Mrs Norris, a perfectly healthy woman who will undoubtedly live to be a hundred, but who summons me regularly, I rather fancy, because nobody else will talk to her on any subject—once went on a visit to Lyme. It was small, she said, and restricted, there was nothing to do and nowhere to go, the people were vulgar and encroaching, the sermons too long—the parson indeed I understood to have had a pronounced stammer—the bathing was exceedingly public, all the houses were poky, all the rooms were minute, even the Assembly Rooms were very small, the concerts few and ill-attended, the whole town smelt of fish—which was, however, excellent when cooked—but even she could admit that, while there, she had never slept better in her life. In short, Madam, she created in me an overwhelming desire to visit Lyme myself—since what Mrs Norris does not like must certainly suit the rest of us. As I am unable to do this in person, I think I must do so *vicariously*. I must ask you to pay my visit for me."

"I do not know Mrs Norris," said Elizabeth, much amused by this, "but I am *well* acquainted with her niece. Such a chapter of complaints from her can only be accepted as a recommendation. And I recall that an aunt of my own went there last year and was quite charmed with it. But—I think only of the problem of our lodgings."

"Well, as to that, I believe a further recommendation may be this. Mrs Norris, who was there in July, informed me that it was *quite* out of season, nobody there at all indeed. I understand the fashionable world gravitates there only in September and October, as the climate is so mild."

"Then—you have convinced me. That is to say, we will see what we can find to lodge in there—and perhaps if we have no luck we can go on to Torbay."

She got up and said: "We are greatly in your debt. Mr Darcy, too, will be most happy to acknowledge this. I can only thank you from my heart."

The doctor also rose and said, smiling again: "I think I can safely say that, once the initial fever was past, I was never in any trepidation. The swift, and complete, recovery of your children, Madam, must be principally owing to yourself. I have occasionally thought, in spite of myself, that the nurse is even more important than the doctor. But nursing is exhausting and I would like, before I go and speaking only as your physician, to recommend you to take a holiday."

He paused for a moment before saying, wooden-faced: "I believe you should go to Lyme."

They laughed together as he went to the door.

"I will do my best to take my physician's advice," said Elizabeth, "and begin to look forward very much to doing so."

Elizabeth relayed this conversation, almost in its entirety, to Mr Darcy when he came upstairs, as he very shortly did. When she had finished he said, simply: "We have never before had occasion to question or doubt the good doctor's advice—I see no reason for doing so now. Mrs Norris dislikes Lyme, Mrs Gardiner delights in it. What further recommendation can we need? It is not a thing I would have thought of without the doctor's suggestion—but, now that he has made it, I begin to wish myself there already."

"Well," said Elizabeth, "I am charmed to find you so decisive. I confess, from what my aunt told me of her visit last year, I have had a thought to go there myself. So now that we are provided with the perfect excuse, how shall we set about it?"

"We shall set about it this very day," said Mr Darcy. "I shall travel post, taking only Patton who, besides being an excellent valet, has always something to say very much to the point on such subjects as lodgings and inns and, especially, servants. Here we are in June, with nearly eighteen hours of daylight. If the roads are not quite as bad as I think they are, beyond Bath, we could arrive there very late tomorrow."

Then, as Elizabeth did not speak—she was indeed much too surprised to do so—he added: "If I fail at Lyme, I will carry on to Sidmouth. The death of the Duke of Kent there, I must suppose some three years ago, did little for its reputation and there may still be elegant lodgings to be had."

Elizabeth put her hand on his arm.

"The only fault I have to find with your excellent plan is—that you must be away from me for ten days or a fortnight. But I think I shall survive it."

"To be sure you will. Let us hope it will prove to be in some sort an adventure—an excursion into the unknown which can only benefit us all. We must not become too staid."

"*Indeed* we must not," said Elizabeth. "Indeed we stand in the *greatest* danger. Here have we been fixed at Pemberley for more than *two months* between adventures. If indeed one must regard London in that light."

Mr Darcy carried her hand to his lips.

"There is never any *need* to be sarcastic, my dearest Elizabeth," he said. "But I hope you may always continue to be so."

"It was that *word*," said Elizabeth. "I can think of no one less staid than yourself—but after four weeks in the nursery I may well begin to have doubts on my own part."

"Then there can be no need for *any*. Let us hope I may be more clever at choosing lodgings than I am at choosing words."

Elizabeth waved him goodbye less than two hours later.

II

Mr Darcy did not keep Elizabeth waiting long for his tidings from Lyme. An express arrived for her in the afternoon, six days after his leaving Pemberley.

My dearest Elizabeth will be pleased to know that her devoted husband has succeeded in his mission beyond his wildest dreams, though his success must be principally owing to the excellent Patton. You and I have more than once suspected that there were eyes in the back of his head. Now I begin to wonder if he has not two other *ears* concealed somewhere about his person. We travelled very expeditiously and not in too much discomfort, putting up here at The Three Cups, about which there is not much to say, either good or bad. On our first evening Patton went to inspect some of the local hostelries and informed me the next morning that a Mr Elgood had some property above the Cobb Hamlet which he was anxious to let, but only to persons "of noble standing". We repaired thither as soon as we had breakfasted, to be greeted by Mr Elgood himself bowing to the ground and calling me "my lord". I put him right on this point as gently, and as quickly, as possible, but did not fail to mention—and this must be quite between ourselves— that there *was* an Earl in the family although I was not he. But I was pleased to observe that he clearly did not believe me and continued his bowing and scraping. It did not take long to decide to hire *all four* of Mr Elgood's houses, which are in a cluster with a fine view of the Cobb and the bay beyond. One house is good, one is indifferent, one is in a state of advanced dilapidation and the fourth can barely stand up by itself. However, by the simple expedient of giving him his rent for two months in advance—it will be an interesting novelty for me to be a tenant—he promises that all will be in order by the first of July. I propose, though, to remain here for at least one other week to make sure that most of the work is done. I am surprised, and pleased, to observe what has been achieved already and visit the houses morning and afternoon taking a *great interest*—which I am even more surprised to find that I actually feel. Patton informs me that Mr Elgood is not much liked in Lyme, being "a furriner outer Charmouth" to use the local dialect. As one can see Charmouth perfectly well from the end of the Cobb, what will they think about *us*, from three hundred miles away in the north? Will they expect icicles dangling from our ears or only *fangs*, do you think? I am in fact quite delighted with everyone here. They are kind and polite but in no way subservient. This may have something to do with the fact that I arrive at the end of every day to make sure that the workmen are paid for that day—by *smiling* at Mr Elgood, you know, and commenting in the most favourable way on the standard of all the work, which I am able to do without in any way impeaching my honour. And now, my love, to business. The houses are none of them large, owing to the lie of the land, and though they have many rooms most of them are extremely small and may, in the summer, be hot and uncomfortable. I doubt there is stabling for more than four horses in any one place in the town and nowhere at all to keep a carriage. Lyme is *steep*. It seems to fall quite vertically into the sea. We must have a butler and a housekeeper, but they must be from among the younger servants. I leave you to explain gracefully to Mrs Reynolds and your Nurse that the hills will be too much for them as this is indeed the case. I think one footman as butler will do quite well but Patton insists that we bring a cook, not necessarily *the* cook. The servants here, he informs me, are only of the most primitive kind. I think we shall need one carriage, which will have to be kept somewhere outside the town, but only two horses and one groom—he can bring them on behind us. I doubt if our coachman would consent to remain behind from such an adventure and perhaps it may be possible for him to lodge wherever I find for the carriage and horses. In short, I am inspired by Lyme. Here we shall spend a summer quite unlike any other. Your journey with the invalids will take about one week. I hope to be with you by 20th June at latest and we should be ready to set out from the 23rd. This comes with all the love of your very devoted Husband.

"So," said Elizabeth aloud, when she had finished reading this, "he has succeeded. We are to go."

She stood up as she spoke, but was surprised by Mrs Reynolds, who had brought her the letter.

"Did you call, madam?" she said.

"No, indeed I did not," replied Elizabeth. "I think I spoke only to myself, but I am most happy that you should still be here. Mr Darcy has found lodgings at Lyme but says he fears the town will be too steep for you and our Nurse and indeed for our butler. He hopes you will not be too disappointed but, reading between the lines, I suspect our accommodations may be somewhat spartan and fit only for the younger ones. He does not say if we should bring our own sheets."

"It is always a wise precaution, madam," said Mrs Reynolds, "and one could scarcely expect a gentleman to think of it. And while I shall be sad not to be with you, there is nowhere more beautiful than Pemberley on a quiet summer's day."

"Do you think that Hannah, the still-room maid, would come with us as housekeeper?"

Mrs Reynolds smiled.

"There is one thing, madam, on which you may entirely depend; and that is that there is no one in this house who would not come with you to the end of the world if that is what you wished."

Elizabeth smiled back.

"Then we shall have no difficulty in finding people to come with us?"

"I think it will be quite the contrary, madam. I foresee the competition will be fierce."

Mrs Reynolds was right. Elizabeth was obliged to exercise what felt, to her, like cruelty, on more than one occasion. She met only token opposition from her Nurse who, after a moment's consideration, paid her the highest compliment of all.

"I think, madam," she said, in a judicial voice, "that you are quite able to look after your own children. But you must take *both* the nurserymaids to assist you."

Elizabeth, who had fully intended to do so, nevertheless bowed graciously and said that she hoped one of them could also help her with her hair? A smiling assent was given by both. She then went on to say that, as there would be little formal entertaining at Lyme, she proposed to take only her simplest dresses and so give her own maid a chance to pay a visit to her mother.

When it was known that the two senior footmen had drawn lots to decree who should go to Lyme as butler, it had to be decided that room must be made for both. Hannah, the still-room maid, glowed with pleasure at the thought of her new responsibilities; and the cook herself, after due deliberation, announced her intention of coming in person. It was no time, she said, to leave her little angels to the mercies of her chief assistant—whose skill with soups and fish were not remarkable, though her puddings and fruit dishes were beyond criticism—and certainly not to the tender care of anyone who might happen to be hired at Lyme.

All these, and many other, arrangements were discussed by Elizabeth with Mrs Reynolds, not least being the provision of adequate containers for the servants' own clothes. Most of them came only from the village and had never had need of such a thing before. The children, even to Elizabeth's perhaps over-critical gaze, seemed to gain strength and colour a little each day; and, in this riot of constant occupation, the ten days were soon gone.

Mr Darcy returned precisely as promised, but he returned alone.

"I trust nothing untoward has overtaken Patton," said Elizabeth, when their greetings had been exchanged.

"Patton, as you might guess, I think, is to be quite the hero of this expedition. I have left him, without a moment's hesitation, in charge of *everything* at Lyme. He will, I have not the slightest doubt, make charming, habitable dwellings out of Mr Elgood's most unpromising properties—and, what is more, when I asked him to do so he looked quite as though I had just given him a hundred pounds, which I now feel very much inclined to do. How fortunate we are, my dearest Elizabeth. What we have gained, the British Army has quite certainly lost. He would have made them all perfectly comfortable even in the middle of Portugal. But I must not neglect *my* duty. Here is a letter from him to Mrs Reynolds, which I am charged to deliver to her within five minutes of my arrival."

Later, when they were alone, he described his journeys to her, saying that he thought six days would be enough for theirs, even though a Sunday intervened. He had bespoken rooms for them already, all along the way, and they would have to leave Pemberley only on the twenty-fourth. Elizabeth, perfectly dazzled by her husband's sudden generalship, found herself with nothing to do beyond ensuring that no favourite garment, or favourite toy, was left behind.

They began their journey exactly as proposed. They travelled in their own carriage, with the children and the two nurserymaids. Behind them, in a hired coach, sat Mrs Maltby, as the cook had now become, and Hannah, housekeeper from that moment. It was an open carriage, piled high with baskets of bedding and with a number of linen bags, strangely shaped and probably, as Elizabeth thought quietly to herself, full of saucepans. Behind them, and in another hired coach, the two footmen, James and John, just contrived to squeeze in beside a quantity of luggage that would certainly have sustained them on a voyage to America.

The whole household assembled on the front steps to wave them farewell, their Nurse's handkerchief sometimes applied to her eyes. As they went down the long drive, the children waved to the herd of goats, which they had previously seen only from their windows.

"Will there be goats at Lyme, Mama?" asked Jane.

"I hope so, my love," replied Elizabeth. "*My* picture of Lyme certainly includes a rather stout lady with a red face and an *enormous* bonnet, who keeps a herd of goats in the fields above the cliffs."

"Will it be an enormous bonnet—big enough to hide Alexander?"

"Well, perhaps not quite that," said Mr Darcy, "but a *very large* sunbonnet. I observed that nearly all the ladies affected this headgear, peculiar to Lyme I thought. Some were larger than others but they were all *huge*," he went on, laughing, "and you shall all of you certainly have one."

"I wish we were at Lyme already," said Anne.

"But we are to have a charming journey," said Elizabeth, "and we are to enjoy it as much as possible. And our enjoyment begins from this moment. I think I have never seen the countryside quite so perfect."

A faultless midsummer shone over England. In the fields, the poppies and corn cockles and corn marigolds bespangled the growing grain; in the hedges the wild roses vied with the elder and honeysuckle to scent the air. Occasionally they passed a field of clover in full flower, most intoxicating of all.

At the first stage they parted with their own horses. Two were to follow behind them to Lyme; two were to return to Pemberley. The grooms were to draw lots on the following day as to which one should go where.

They slept that night at Ashby-de-la-Zouch and the next at Kenilworth. Here the children were obliged to sleep together in one bed, which so delighted them all that they did so every night thereafter. The inns were clean and comfortable and the food, to Elizabeth's relief and surprise, was both well-cooked and well-seasoned, quite beyond her expectation.

Friday brought them to the White Hart at Bath, where Mr Darcy had promised her a pleasant surprise; and this turned out to be the company of Lady Alicia and Mrs Frankland at dinner.

Elizabeth was truly delighted. They had become acquainted three years previously, through the agency of Elizabeth's aunt Gardiner, a schoolfriend of Mrs Frankland's. Elizabeth had been in Bath with her father, after the death of her mother, and a true friendship had grown up. Lady Alicia and Mrs Frankland had visited Pemberley later that same summer and again in the summer that followed.

They were sisters-in-law, married to brothers, both of whom had been killed in the long war against France. They had set up house together as widows, living in Bath in Laura Place, and had remained in mourning until the death of the Emperor Napoleon. They had then cast off their widows' weeds, given a series of rout parties and a ball, and had continued, for one reason or another, in a subdued state of excitement and enjoyment ever since. Mrs Frankland maintained a regular correspondence with Mrs Gardiner, who maintained a regular correspondence with Elizabeth.

III

I t was two years since they had met but those years vanished in an instant in the warmth of their greeting.

"My dear, dear Elizabeth," said Lady Alicia, coming into the room first, "how entranced we were—can it have been only last week?—to see your charming husband again and to hear that we would be shortly seeing you *all*."

"And it is such a pleasure to see you looking so *well*," said Mrs Frankland. "We quite thought, hearing all the sad news from the sick room at Pemberley, to find you a *shadow* of your former self."

"On that head," said Elizabeth, when she had kissed them both, "I think at one time I was looking a little *wan*—but as all the arrangements for our present expedition have been made by my excellent husband, I have been resting, and recovering, for very nearly three weeks."

Mr Darcy shook hands with them, remarked on their radiant looks, and then they all sat down.

"But you must tell me at once," said Elizabeth, "before they come in with the dinner, what news do you have of all our Bath acquaintance? I am particularly interested to know—though I cannot precisely tell you why—what has become of Lady Elliot?"

The two ladies exchanged a knowing glance, their smiles broadening almost into laughter.

"You could hardly have chosen a more invigorating topic," said Lady Alicia. "Our information is only newly arrived in Bath as well."

"Sir Walter had no trouble with his divorce, you know," said Mrs Frankland, "and it was all paid for with Tilney money, just as we expected."

"But then, of course, we all thought that Colonel Tilney would *marry* Lady Elliot. Only—he did not!"

"They went at first to Italy, quite in the accepted mode, like Byron and Shelley and everyone else. And then he *deserted* her! Quite literally, you know. Walked out one morning, leaving her with what was left of the family jewellery."

"The rest of which," added Lady Alicia, nodding her head, "had never been given back by the Colonel's step-mother, Sir Walter's elder daughter, of course."

"Then I feel quite sorry for the Colonel," said Mr Darcy. "What has become of him?"

"Oh, he is now back at Northanger, making life impossible for all around him, just as his father did before him."

"There is no need to waste your sympathy on him," said Mrs Frankland. "To elope with a woman of Lady Elliot's stamp is *not* the mark of a sensible man."

"So Lady Elliot is still in Italy?" said Elizabeth. "I wonder how she goes on."

"There is no need to worry about her either," remarked Lady Alicia. "You may depend upon it, she has already found someone there to defray her expenses."

"And those poor little boys?" asked Elizabeth. "Three, I think?"

"Well, there I must agree with you," said Mrs Frankland. "*They* are to be pitied in all conscience. They are at Kellynch Hall, with their foolish father and their half-sister, Mrs General Tilney, a sour-faced young woman if ever I saw one. I can only hope there are some congenial servants in that house."

"But the great comfort is that their very existence prevents the reversion of the baronetcy—for even Sir Walter cannot live for ever—to Mr William Elliot, a cold-hearted, formal man who once made eyes at our great friend Anne Elliot. We were quite afraid, at one time, you know, that she would marry him."

"But she married a very dashing—would not you say that Admiral Wentworth, as he now is, was dashing, Alicia?—naval officer instead. And we were all much relieved."

"Except, I must suppose, Mr William Elliot?" said Mr Darcy. "I feel obliged to put in a word on behalf of my own sex."

"As to *that*," said Lady Alicia, positively, "you need waste no sympathy on *him*. A man whose sole consideration is for himself can *never* be an object of compassion."

"No doubt he is at this very moment plotting the deaths of those three little boys," said Mrs Frankland, with the slightest inclination of her head, "but I think they are really too *many* for him."

By now, the dinner began to be brought in, and the conversation settled into less sensational channels. They discussed the weather, the Gardiners, the deplorable politics of the French and the newest jewels of Lady Conyngham with both spirit and invention. The dinner, Elizabeth thought, had been particularly well-chosen. She found herself glancing at Mr Darcy, who had been responsible for this, with increasing frequency and appreciation.

When the servants had gone, and they had returned to their sitting-room for tea and coffee, Mr Darcy said: "There is another person in whom both Elizabeth and I continue to feel an interest, Lady Alicia. Perhaps you can tell us something about her—Miss Crawford?"

"Oh dear," said Lady Alicia, putting down her cup. "There are only sad tidings there. I scarcely know where to begin."

"We last heard of her in Norfolk, with Mrs Grant, trying to bring their brother to his senses," said Elizabeth. "One can only hope that they succeeded?"

"I fear not so," said Lady Alicia. "Indeed I feel so very *sad* for her. She did not deserve all the disasters that descended on her head."

Elizabeth began to feel a little alarmed.

"You must not take my sister's gloomy words too much to heart," said Mrs Frankland. "She did not at all succeed with her brother who died—in rather mysterious circumstances, you know, some thought by his own hand—in the first half of last year. She wrote to us, in great distress, about that time."

"And then, like the redoubtable young woman that she is," continued Lady Alicia, "she set to and put both house and estate in order—not that she could do that completely in six months—and it is now let, not to an Admiral as Kellynch Hall once was, but to a General of the East India Company."

"Since Michaelmas last year," said Mrs Frankland, "and we have not heard from her since. Our letters to her at Everingham at Christmas were returned."

"I noticed the death of an Admiral Crawford in the paper not so long ago," said Mr Darcy. "It mentioned Everingham as a boyhood home."

"Her uncle, without a doubt," said Lady Alicia. "There was an aunt as well, if you recall, but I think she died some time ago."

"If all this money has devolved upon *her*," said Mrs Frankland, "she must now be very rich. But where can she be, do you think? Is there a new spa somewhere, where she is to be found with Mrs Grant? One feels so helpless, so totally useless."

"Then let us hope she is to be found at Lyme," said Elizabeth, lightly. "The sea-bathing would certainly be of benefit to Mrs Grant."

The two ladies sat up immediately.

"It is *more* than a possibility," said Lady Alicia.

"You must keep your eyes *wide open*," said Mrs Frankland.

"I hope you will like Lyme," said Lady Alicia, a bit doubt-fully. "Opinions seem to vary. In Bath there are Lyme people and Sidmouth people—though as *all* the protagonists are rather disagreeable one does not attempt to take sides."

"We ourselves say we are Weymouth people. We went there once—did we not, Alicia?—and disliked it extremely."

Elizabeth could not help smiling.

"Well, indeed, I hope that you may become Lyme people, like ourselves," she said. "Would it be too much to ask you to visit us there in—shall we say—about three weeks time?"

"Most certainly it would not," said Lady Alicia, with her widest smile.

"*Nothing* could give us more pleasure," said Mrs Frankland, at the same time.

"But *one thing* I must warn you against," said Lady Alicia, in some amusement. "Lyme, you know, has the reputation of being full of unattached females *of a certain age*. It is supposed to be the end of the road if you are looking for a husband."

It was Mr Darcy's turn to smile.

"I am already quite terrified," he said. "Elizabeth, you must promise never to let me out without you."

"I will certainly promise you that," said Elizabeth, very happily. "Even if Miss Bingley *is* lurking there already."

"An unlikely contingency," said Mr Darcy, almost shortly, adding a moment or two later, "I hope."

As the ladies rose to take their leave, Elizabeth said: "I am not too sure of our accommodations, I must confess. But with three weeks to arrange it, we can be certain to offer you *some* comfort."

"And you must remember," said Mrs Frankland, "that we are Army wives, living together in Lisbon in the greatest *dis*comfort—can it be ten years ago, Alicia?"

"It can indeed. And I often think of them as three of the happiest years of our lives."

"Then," said Elizabeth, "I depend on seeing you there very soon. I will write at once when I am satisfied that Lyme is not to be too like Lisbon."

IV

They left Bath in the late morning on the following day, travelling only as far as Sherborne, where they were to spend the Sunday. They attended Matins in the Abbey, their whole party filling two pews, and substantially increasing the volume of sound made by the congregation. The inn was comfortable, but there was little to do except wander, the weather remaining fine and dry.

They were off immediately after breakfast the next day and came to Lyme while the sun was still high in the afternoon. The road to Mr Elgood's houses was so steep that they left the carriages at some distance above them, on the Sidmouth Road, and walked down the rest of the way.

There were some fine trees, particularly some notable ash, so that their first sight of the sea did not appear quite at once. Then, almost suddenly, they were looking over the harbour, over the fishing boats lying within the shelter of the Cobb, over the sea itself, sparklingly calm, and, far beyond, to the hills of Dorset arching their way to the Chesil Bank, the eastern bastions of Lyme Bay. It was a view to take the breath away, and their exclamations of admiration were loud and long.

Mr Elgood's houses seemed, from above, to be liable to slip down the hill, poised as they were on a kind of shoulder, facing over the Cobb and towards the west. They were not large. Indeed, by any previous standards, Elizabeth thought them very small and wondered how they were all to fit in; but they were welcomed so smilingly by Patton and, later, by Mr Elgood himself, that she decided to remain silent on that head.

In the largest house they were to live themselves, with Patton and the two nurserymaids. The second house, just below it, had been entirely prepared for the reception of guests, with three very good bedrooms and its own sitting room. The two others, though the painting outside had yet to be completed, proved unexpectedly spacious. In the first one there were rooms for Hannah and Mrs Maltby, with a kitchen and a room where all the servants could eat; and in the second, the one which Mr Darcy had described as being almost unable to stand up by itself—but which had now been shored up, made weatherproof and painted—there were just two rooms, one up and one down, for the two footmen. The coachman and the groom, when he arrived, were to lodge at the farm where the horses and the carriage were to be kept.

While they were inspecting these accommodations, their baggages were being brought down, and calmly despatched, on Patton's instructions, to their respective quarters. Mr Darcy walked back up the hill to pay off the various postilions and to direct the coachman to his new abode; and while he was doing so, Elizabeth found herself addressed by Patton.

"I have ventured, madam," he said, in his most correct manner, "to bespeak a dinner for my master and yourself—and for the children should you wish it—at the inn below, which you may see from this window. I did not think it would be possible to provide a meal worthy of your consumption so soon after your arrival."

"That seems an excellent plan, I think, and very well thought of. We will take the children with us."

"I have engaged a good plain cook to work in what I may call House Number Three. She will have a dinner ready for the servants. I only hope it may not prove beneath the notice of Mrs Maltby herself."

"I hope it may not, indeed. But I think that an excellent arrangement. Mrs Maltby and Hannah may, in general, spend the day up here. I hope there is somewhere for them to sit? Two women in two kitchens is much to be preferred. Let us not forget we are come for a holiday—so must keep all strife to a minimum."

"My thoughts exactly, madam. I am sure this visit to Lyme will benefit us all. There was just one other matter."

"Of course."

"It is about what I must call transport in Lyme. You will have observed, madam, how extremely steep the road is outside this house. One may walk, or go by donkey—since they are more sure-footed than the horse—or take a sedan-chair or a one-horse cart, which one may drive oneself. As the distances are so small—one can indeed master the whole topography of the town in twenty minutes—I was not certain which you would wish to do."

"I think," said Elizabeth, after a moment, "that I would wish to walk. The children, I have no doubt, will wish to go by donkey. But I am more concerned for Hannah and Mrs Maltby. I understand the market to be in Broad Street, at some distance?"

"I will approach them separately, madam. Should you wish to attend the Assembly Rooms, a sedan-chair will be advisable."

"I begin to realise that Lyme is not quite like anywhere else."

"No, madam, it is not. It has a charm that nowhere else can match and I foresee a stay of unalloyed pleasure for us all. I will escort you to the inn, madam, when you should be ready, and James, or John, will ensure your safe return."

The walk down to the inn occupied no more than five minutes. As it seemed probable that they would be eating together as a family for much of the time at Lyme, Elizabeth invited the two nurserymaids to come with them. They were sisters, native to Pemberley village, who had devotedly nursed the three children through their illness.

Their devotion was abundantly returned. Baptised Rebecca and Jemima, they were known to the children as Becca and Mima, and no expedition was complete without at least one of them.

Welcomed by the landlord, they were seated at a large round table and the dinner, once more of an excellence quite surprising to Elizabeth, was served immediately.

There were only two other people in the room where they were dining, seated by a window which offered an uninterrupted view of the harbour. They were a little older than herself and Mr Darcy, dressed with an elegant plainness that proclaimed their taste and assurance. They looked up as the family arrived, but did not stare. When they left the room, both inclined their heads and the woman wished them "Goodnight", a wish which Elizabeth returned.

She was seized with an overwhelming desire to know who they were, but determined to restrain her curiosity. While one question to the landlord would have satisfied her, she did not want to appear vulgarly inquisitive. No doubt Patton would be able to enlighten her.

Included in their final course was a goat cheese of peculiar excellence, and they ate it all. This time there could be no objection to consulting the landlord, who had served the dinner himself, and she said to him: "I hope that cheese may be local, landlord, as I would wish to eat a great deal more of it."

"It is, madam, it is indeed," replied the landlord, beaming. "It is a Mrs Wicken makes it and she brings it to me fresh each day."

"Does she have an *enormous* bonnet?" asked Jane.

"Well, now that you ask me, little miss, I believe she does. She lives right over the Ware Cleeves, just afore the forest."

"Do you think she could also supply us with milk? I should be happy to purchase any she might have to spare."

"Most certainly I will ask her tomorrow, madam. I make no mistake that she will be most pleased to assist you."

"At Mr Elgood's house, then. She may ask for Mrs Maltby."

Mr Darcy settled their account; they complimented the cook on her skill and the landlord bowed them out, expressing the hope that they would again favour him with their custom.

"There can be no doubt about that," said Mr Darcy. "We are fortunate to have you so close."

Their way home was short, but very steep. Alexander was swung up the hill between his father and James. Elizabeth took a hand of each of her daughters, with Rebecca and Jemima on the outside. They arrived at their front door only very slightly out of breath.

They were greeted by Patton.

"It will not take you long to get used to the hills, madam," he said. "In my weeks of residence here I have developed a new pair of legs, and would most respectfully advise you to do the same."

Elizabeth smiled and said she would most certainly make the attempt. As she sat upstairs, brushing her hair before going to bed, she had leisure to think what a pleasant day it had been and, in particular, how agreeable all the local inhabitants appeared to be.

She slept exceptionally well.

V

As their bedroom overlooked the New Road, Elizabeth was wakened the next morning by a commotion. She reached the window just in time to witness the departure of a most interesting cavalcade. Mrs Maltby, balanced on the back of a donkey, was accompanied by a second donkey, burdened only by two empty pannier baskets. Beside her walked Hannah and the footman James, while John walked on her other side to be at hand, Elizabeth supposed, should she happen to slide off.

After a moment's wonder about the fate of her own breakfast, Elizabeth turned to Mr Darcy to find him gone. He must have got out of bed very quietly not to have woken her. Putting on her wrapper, she went at once to the nursery where, to her astonishment, she found the children having breakfast.

"Have I overslept?" she asked Rebecca. "Surely it is still very early?"

"It is very early, madam," replied Rebecca, smiling, "but the sun was so bright and so soon in at our windows, that I could not keep us in bed a moment longer."

"Mr Patton thought it best we should breakfast up here," said Jemima, "being as how breakfast is sometimes a bit messy. There is a staircase straight to the kitchen."

"I think that an excellent scheme," said Elizabeth. "Truly, he has thought of everything."

She kissed the children, asked Jemima to come in ten minutes to help her with her hair, and twenty-five minutes later descended to the dining-room, amazed to discover that it was not yet half-past eight.

She greeted Patton, who awaited her there, and asked if he knew where Mr Darcy was.

"He went out some time ago, madam. I understood him to say he would walk on the beach for a short time. I will bring in the breakfast directly."

"I saw Mrs Maltby setting off on her donkey," said Elizabeth, with as little expression in her voice as she could achieve.

"I am glad to say, madam," said Patton, understanding her perfectly, "that Mrs Maltby was so pleased with the dinner that Mrs Sidford cooked for her last night that she was willing to entrust the preparation of your breakfast to Mrs Sidford, while she went to the market herself. Though I am inclined to suppose that, by tomorrow, those roles may be reversed. Mrs Maltby did not look quite comfortable upon her donkey and Mrs Sidford must already know where the best provisions are to be found."

"I think that very possible," said Elizabeth, with a smile. "And I must hope you do not dislike *your* new role as general guardian of us all?"

"No, indeed, madam," said Patton, but without a smile. "Mr Darcy cannot require my normal services here for more than half-an-hour a day, except on first-rate occasions. I am more than happy to be otherwise occupied."

"Certainly Lyme is no place for standing on ceremony. Indeed, there is scarcely room to do so, and I believe I shall thrive upon its informality. I must hope that Mr Darcy will do so too."

"As you say, madam. I will bring in your rolls immediately."

Elizabeth had no more than poured her second cup of coffee than she was joined by Mr Darcy, only slightly dishevelled from his walk along the beach.

"My love," he said, kissing the top of her head, "I scarcely expected to see you down so early. I cannot remember when we last breakfasted together. I believe this must only be one of the improvements that Lyme will bring into our lives."

"I was awoken by the bustle made by Mrs Maltby, setting off for the market upon a donkey," said Elizabeth, very seriously.

"How sad I am to have been denied so interesting a sight," said Mr Darcy, a laugh in his voice, "and with nothing much to compensate for it. The Monmouth Beach is a sad place, after all, a mass of uncomfortable little rocks and quite large stones. It was where the unfortunate Duke landed, you know, in 1685, I rather think, and where many of his men were later hanged. There is still a gloom about it, even on a day like this. I believe it to be quite haunted, in fact, and do not mean to trespass there again."

"Have you some thoughts of how we should start the day?"

"I am in no doubt of that at all. Our first port of call must be the sunbonnet shop."

Elizabeth took the time to write to her sister Catherine at Torbay, to give her their direction at Lyme, and to express the hope that they would contrive a meeting in the course of the summer. That done, she put on her bonnet, collected the children and the nurserymaids, and was then delighted to find that Mr Darcy chose to come with them, the two footmen being not yet returned from the market.

Their way lay behind the bathing beach, the tide being at that moment very low. Most of the machines had been drawn out to it and sheeted figures could be seen jumping up and down in the water.

"I think we might wait a day or two," said Mr Darcy, "until the sea approaches us a little more nearly. Though by this afternoon it should be suiting us better. I hope you mean to bathe?"

"Most certainly I do," said Elizabeth, "and the children as well. I understand we must bespeak our machine the day before, for a certain time. Patton tells me the second one from this end, the one with the blue-and-white stripes, is the one to choose, and Mrs Tegg is the bathing-woman."

"Has Patton been into the sea, then?" asked Mr Darcy in some surprise.

"That he did not tell me, but I am no longer able to be amazed by any of Patton's activities. And I shall most certainly take his advice."

They went first to the Receiving Office in Coombe Street, to deposit Catherine's letter, and then to the milliner's in Broad Street. Here all the females in the party were equipped with sunbonnets, wide and shady at the front and with a flap to cover the back of the neck. A straw hat was obtained for Alexander and they then turned towards home. The road behind the bathing beach was neither very good nor very bad and Elizabeth was astonished to realise, when they reached the bottom of the New Road, that she had now walked almost the entire length of the sea-front at Lyme.

As the tide was still a long way out, they decided to walk along the Cobb, joined to the land only by a kind of causeway. The Cobb was a long sea-wall, snaking its way away, sheltering the harbour from the south-west. It was built at two levels, the upper perhaps six feet higher than the lower, and several flights of dangerous-looking steps gave access from one to the other. Farther out, a Y was made by a new extension and, in the angle of this, a little sandy beach had been left by the receding tide.

As they neared the end of the Cobb, Jane, who missed very little, pointed and said: "Look, Mama—D'Arcy."

A plaque had been let in to the wall and Jane, with occasional help from Elizabeth, read it aloud.

The work extending 275 yards west of this stone was erected by James Hamilton Builder & Contractor with the Honble Board of Ordnance to repair the Breaches made in the Cobb in January 1792 under the direction of Capt D'Arcy Engineer 1793

"Why do they only put Capt for Captain, Mama?" asked Jane. "And what does Honble mean?"

"I fancy they had not quite space enough for all the words, my love. Honble is short for Honourable. Everything at Lyme is just a little cramped, you know, but"—turning to Mr Darcy— "I have never quite had the courage to enquire when your family abandoned their apostrophe."

"I rather think they never had one," said Mr Darcy, at his most amiable. "The deeds of Pemberley go back only to 1549, when a certain Mortimer Darcy—without an apostrophe—purchased the original estate from the Crown. He is described as a merchant, from Boston in Lincolnshire, and the assumption is that he traded mostly in Denmark and Holland. Perhaps our Darcys came from there. My father would tease my mother by saying that the moors of Northumberland, where she came from herself, were full of wild Darcys, so savage and poor that they scarcely wore clothes, but she could never be brought to believe it. No doubt Captain D'Arcy Engineer came from France, or from some softer southern branch of the family. I am sure the wild northern Darcys would have thought an apostrophe a fearful affectation—and indeed I am rather inclined to think it that myself."

"Nevertheless, the heroic action of Captain D'Arcy Engineer, however soft and southern he may have been, in extending the Cobb by two hundred and seventy-five yards, makes me feel that we belong here—we are involved with Lyme. Already, after less than a day, I feel myself to be quite a resident."

"It is a charming place, indeed," said Mr Darcy. "I was quite certain you would like it. And not the least of its charms, for me, is that, while we are here, no one knows us as the Darcys of Pemberley—we are under no obligation to anyone and may behave exactly as we please. Though not, you may be relieved to hear, to the extent of purchasing a straw hat like Alexander's for myself, as I was sorely tempted to do this morning. I felt a little foolish on the Monmouth Beach in my Pemberley hat, you know. Though perhaps an outfitter *here* might still have a round hat from twenty years ago, laid down upon some dusty shelf. I will apply myself to that problem tomorrow."

"But even if they can find one," said Elizabeth, "you may be sure it will be extremely heavy—made of felt or serge or shoddy or some such thing. Is it not the kind of hat that farmers wear in winter to keep off the rain? You would be better advised, I think, if you can come by one, to have the sunbonnet shop copy it in straw."

"Now that, indeed, is an inspiration entirely worthy of you and it is exactly what I shall do. And not tomorrow either, but this very afternoon."

As they passed the little beach in the arms of the Cobb, Elizabeth found herself wishing to take off her shoes and paddle in the sea. Then, fortunately, she recollected that it was time to be home for their nuncheon.

"But I *quite* agree with you," said Mr Darcy, smiling at Elizabeth with his eyes. "I have only ever paddled in the stream at Pemberley, but the temptation is overwhelming, I admit. Perhaps we may be able to give in to it another day—though I fear this beach is covered at high tide."

As they made their way back along the lower Cobb, they could see the people who had dined at the inn the night before walking along the top. A kind of bow passed between the ladies; the gentlemen raised their hats; and Elizabeth found herself wishing more than ever that she could make their acquaintance.

She did not forget to consult Patton about the bathing-machine on her return, but a disappointment awaited her here.

"I regret, madam, that tomorrow is not a ladies' day for bathing. Their days are Tuesdays, Thursdays and Saturdays. The gentlemen have the other days and there is no bathing on Sundays, except for accredited invalids, and in the baths."

"I think we passed some baths as we left the Cobb Hamlet?"

"Yes, madam, those are England's Baths. Mr Davie's Baths are at quite the other side of the town, almost overlooking the Church Cliffs."

"So Mr Darcy must bathe alone tomorrow?"

"He could take Master Alexander, I am sure, if Master Alexander should wish to go. He is in the happy position of being able to bathe every day of the week, being old enough to do so with his father, and young enough to do so with his mother."

"We must reserve the machine of Mrs Tegg for two hours every day. As we have come here for our health we cannot neglect it. But there are very few bathing-machines, in fact—hardly more than half-a-dozen."

"The beach is quite small, as you will have noticed, madam, which I understand is why mixed bathing is not to be encouraged. But James shall speak to Mrs Tegg. Might I suggest eleven o'clock in the morning as being a good time?"

Elizabeth acquiesced, after only a moment's hesitation, and then went upstairs to take off her bonnet. Mrs Maltby had returned safely from her hazardous expedition and a nuncheon awaited them in the dining-room.

VI

Mr Darcy came home in triumph shortly after one o'clock on the following day, bearing in his arms a glowing Alexander, who had been totally immersed in the sea—which he had thought the greatest joke in the world—and, on his head, an extremely handsome round straw hat, which had been made for him overnight in the sun-bonnet shop.

There were no other topics of conversation for the rest of the day. The exhilaration of the sea water, the excitement of the waves, the exceptional skill of the straw hat makers, the excessive amiability of everyone at Lyme, were enough. They walked on the Cobb again in the afternoon, with the children and both the nurserymaids, but the little beach was covered by the tide.

"I fear it is too deep to paddle," they remarked almost simultaneously, and joined in their laughter together.

There was another, larger, beach by the harbour, where several skiffs and bumboats, dinghies and small rowing-boats, lay until floated by the incoming tide. They walked among these before deciding that they were, in fact, too easily to be seen by the general public were they to take their shoes off *here*. The beach in the arms of the Cobb would be almost completely private, save for actual walkers on the Cobb.

"Well," said Elizabeth stoically, "perhaps we shall be more lucky tomorrow. We will come a little earlier."

It now emerged that not only had Rebecca and Jemima no intention of bathing in the sea, but they had also no intention of putting even their feet into it. Elizabeth merely smiled.

"I hope that, when you see how much we enjoy it, and of how much benefit it is to us, you may be persuaded to change your minds."

So she went by herself with her children to Mrs Tegg's machine at eleven o'clock the next day, escorted by James and by Mr Darcy himself. Rebecca and Jemima, convinced that they would never see them again, accepted the escort of John to the end of the Cobb, from where an excellent view of any distant tragedy might be obtained.

They were no sooner inside the machine than it began to move, trundling over the wet sand and pebbles in fairly erratic progression. Their motive force was a small pony, beside which walked the gigantic Mrs Tegg, her natural size even enhanced by her huge bonnet and vast skirt. These she continued to wear, to Elizabeth's admiring amazement, when she went into the sea up to her waist.

Elizabeth had been warned that no bathing clothes were supplied for children, so Jane and Anne and Alexander went into the sea in their night clothes. She herself, arrayed in what looked much like a shroud—though it was made of flannel rather than linen—and with a considerable turban on her head, was secretly pleased that no one she knew could possibly see her in this very extraordinary costume.

The machine stopped. They opened the door. Mrs Tegg said something which Elizabeth thought was probably "Come you in, me darlins" and they walked down the steps into the sea.

It was surprisingly warm. Mrs Tegg took firm hold of Alexander and Anne, while Jane and Elizabeth, hand in hand, ventured a little further out, until Jane, standing, and Elizabeth, kneeling, were up to their necks in the water. There was no wind. Little waves lapped against them, sometimes splashing their faces. They tried floating, but were weighed down by the bulk of their clothing. Then the children discovered a new game, to go up to the top step of the machine and jump off, caught by Elizabeth or by Mrs Tegg, who held them on the surface of the water, encouraging them to move both arms and legs as though they were swimming.

In this way an hour was soon passed. It was not until the waves began to cover the top step that Mrs Tegg said it was best to be gone now; and they all went back into the machine to change out of their bathing clothes.

There was only one other machine out as far as theirs, the occupant apparently a lone woman. She started to ascend the steps of her machine at the same time as Elizabeth was ascending hers and, though she was some way off, Elizabeth turned to look at her. Her glance was returned; and Elizabeth froze. They paused. Despite their turbans and their shrouds, complete internal recognition passed between them. Then, as though released by a spring, they both sought refuge in the gloom and safety of their machines.

"Who was that lady, Mama?" asked Jane, observant as ever, as soon as the door was closed.

"Miss Bingley, my darling, your uncle Bingley's sister," said Elizabeth, amazed by her own composure.

"Is she the one who is always nasty to aunt Jane? Elizabeth— my cousin Elizabeth, you know, not you, Mama—says they are always at daggers drawn, which is a very rude expression is it not?"

"Very rude indeed, my love, but I hope it may not be true. She is quite the last person whom I wished to see here, on our holiday."

She had dressed the children, and herself after a fashion, by the time the machine was returned to the beach. The children were noisily and joyously welcomed by Rebecca and Jemima, as though they had been absent for several weeks, and she herself was greeted by Mr Darcy.

"My dearest Elizabeth," he immediately said. "Have you seen a ghost? You are quite pale."

"Oh, if only that were so, indeed. How welcome a ghost would be. But it is even more alarming, I can assure you."

She paused, to catch her breath.

"Miss Bingley *is* here," she said, in an urgent undertone.

Mr Darcy did not speak.

"She is in the end machine," Elizabeth went on, "the one nearest to the town. And she has seen me. I have hustled on my clothes all anyhow, as you may observe, so that we may be well upon our way before she comes out."

Mr Darcy put his arm under hers and quickened his step. By the time they reached the bottom of the New Road they were practically running, neither of them daring to look back.

"At least," said Elizabeth, as they began to climb the hill up to their house, "she is not lodging at this end of the town. I have been here long enough to know that the Cobb Hamlet is considered quite out of the way. No doubt that is why we like it so much, but it would not suit Miss Bingley."

"When last we heard of her, and her sister, surely they were in Italy? Did not Jane, your sister Jane, tell us they had wintered at Leghorn?"

"My little joke at Bath has rebounded upon me, with a vengeance indeed, when Lady Alicia told us that Lyme was the last resort of old maids. And certainly she was with her sister at Leghorn, which was why the house in Grosvenor Street was empty and Jane and Mr Bingley could give their ball."

"Well, there is no understanding it—yet," said Mr Darcy philosophically. "But as we are bound to meet her somewhere, we had better accustom our minds to encountering the unavoidable."

It took Elizabeth some time to regain her customary calm. Miss Bingley was a person she could never like, her manners so cold, so calculated and so correct. But at the same time she could still give the impression that she considered Mr Darcy would have done better to have married her, rather than Elizabeth. They did not even catch a glimpse of her during the rest of the week, and Elizabeth was able to banish her, at least to the back of her mind.

Mr Darcy went riding on the mornings that he did not bathe. His horses were stabled, and the carriage was housed, at a farm some two miles from the town. In the afternoons they walked, on the Cobb or on the cliffs above it, finding a delightful grassy path leading to woods, the main footpath to Seaton.

They attended morning service as a family, in the Parish Church on Sunday, accompanied by the footmen and the nurserymaids. It was a walk of little more than fifteen minutes, accomplished in bright sunshine. They occupied the best part of one of the long pews and were scarcely seated when a woman, whom Elizabeth could clearly recognise as Miss Bingley even from behind, came in alone. Elizabeth quietly determined to exercise all her best powers of Christian tolerance during the service, so that she might meet Miss Bingley with equanimity at the end of it.

But she was not to be so fortunate. Miss Bingley had walked confidently up to a particular pew, only to find it already full. She looked round and spotted Mr Darcy in his seat next to the aisle. Approaching him directly she said, with a glittering smile: "Would you do me the kindness to let me in beside you? Some strangers have stolen my pew."

There was no escape. Miss Bingley placed herself firmly between Mr Darcy and Elizabeth, ostentatiously kneeling to pray just as the service began. Elizabeth could manage no more than a most reluctant smile when they turned towards each other. The text for the sermon, when it came, was: "Thou shalt love thy neighbour as thyself".

VII

Elizabeth, cradling Alexander as he slumbered quietly through that sermon, found herself a little disappointed by the church of St Michael the Archangel. She had hoped for some visible reminder of the great days of Lyme, when it had been one of the principal ports of England; but there was nothing to distract the eye, or even particularly to please it. The pews were hard and the impression given was of a place of worship more than usually austere.

By the end of the service, she was sufficiently braced to encounter Miss Bingley, though in no very Christian spirit, in spite of, or perhaps because of, the sermon. Consigning the children to the care of the servants, and suggesting that they left the church through the door in the north aisle, she followed Mr Darcy and Miss Bingley out of the west door, fully intending to accept any offer of refreshment that Miss Bingley might choose to make, while sadly reflecting, at the same time, that all their comfort in being at Lyme must now be at an end.

Miss Bingley did not disappoint her. Addressing herself to Mr Darcy, she said: "I hope you will do me the honour, and give me the pleasure, of a visit to my house, which is only just over the road."

Turning to Elizabeth, and adjusting her smile a little, she said: "You may easily see it from here."

She led the way, down Monmouth Street. Miss Bingley's house was Monmouth House which, as she was not slow to inform them, once they were inside it, was quite the best house to be had in the whole of Lyme.

"Do not you find, Miss Elizabeth, that your residence in the Cobb Hamlet is sadly out of the way?" she asked, with a widening smile.

"Our decision to spend the summer at Lyme," replied Mr Darcy at his most imposing, "was only made quite lately, on the advice, in fact, of our physician, our children having had the misfortune to contract the scarlet fever. I consider myself extremely lucky to have discovered our present lodgings at such a late date because our household, as you know, is not a small one."

"I am so sorry to hear," said Miss Bingley, retracting her smile a short distance, "that your children have been unwell. I trust no lasting damage, and that they are by now perfectly recovered?"

"Perfectly, I thank you," said Elizabeth, quite mesmerised by the excellence of Miss Bingley's teeth. "We believe goat's milk to have been the saving grace. They drank it every day, and we bathed their faces with it, so that now, I am happy to say, there is not a blemish to be seen. But I hope you mean to tell us, dear Miss Bingley," she went on, suddenly seizing the initiative, "how it is that you come to be in Lyme yourself. When last we heard, you were in Italy. And is the house in London quite shut up?"

Miss Bingley's smile vanished completely.

"I trust there is no bad news in your family," remarked Mr Darcy, into the ensuing silence.

"No, no, indeed," said Miss Bingley, rather hastily. "My sister has been obliged—that is to say, her house in London has been let—to Colonel and Lady Alethea Gordon."

The names were mentioned in that tone of voice which indicated that everyone should certainly know who *they* were. Elizabeth, perfectly satisfied that she had never heard of either, contented herself by remarking, in a voice which sounded, even to herself, a trifle patronising: "I am sure they will make excellent tenants."

Then, after a moment, she said: "But your sister, Mrs Hurst? She is not here with you at Lyme?"

Miss Bingley did not immediately reply. The signs of inner conflict made themselves visible, her breathing slightly quickened, her right hand fastened hard upon the arm of her chair.

"My sister," she said at last, "remains in Italy. She has formed—my sister has formed—my sister has formed an unfortunate—my sister has formed an unfortunate passion—my sister has formed an unfortunate passion for Lord Byron."

"I hope you do not mean to tell us," said Mr Darcy at his driest, "that this passion is returned?"

"I do not, indeed," said Miss Bingley, "though there are times that I might wish that it were, such misery does it seem to cause her. Wherever he goes, she must follow, though I am happy to say, at present, that he seems to be fixed at Leghorn. Travelling in Italy, you know," half her smile appearing once again, "is very costly."

"And is she quite alone at Leghorn?" asked Elizabeth. "I am surprised that you should have deserted her in her hour of need."

"As to that," said Miss Bingley, even her half-smile now disappearing entirely, "it was at her own request. She knew how very unhappy I was, observing her hopeless attachment. And then she had recently made the acquaintance of a certain Lady Elliot, whom I could not like, but who was prepared to share her sorrows, and, to an extent, her feelings."

"And her income, perhaps, as well?" remarked Mr Darcy. "If she is the Lady Elliot who is very slightly known to us, I can see that that might be the case."

"Perceptive of you, indeed," said Miss Bingley, all archness of manner suddenly extinguished. "But then I have always known you as a very percipient man."

A servant now brought in some lemonade and sponge cakes; and the consumption of these occupied their attention completely, for some time.

Monmouth House looked out on to a little green, where two beautiful white goats were grazing greedily. There was no view of the sea, except perhaps from the upper floors. Elizabeth could not understand what made it so desirable.

"You are quite enclosed here," she said easily. "Perhaps Mr Elgood's houses err somewhat in the other direction. But it is a charming house indeed, and I must hope you are very happy here."

"It dates, I believe, from before the Rebellion of the Duke of Monmouth. The panelling, as you may see, is of a very superior kind. But I think I may confess to you that there was little else that I could hire. I do not mean to remain beyond the end of August."

Then, after a moment, she added: "My brother Charles invites me for September."

If there was a challenge in her voice as she said this, Elizabeth chose to ignore it. She was unable to ask directly why Miss Bingley had selected Lyme for her summer residence—that, she thought, might be a little too enquiring. But Lady Alicia's words continued to reverberate in her head and she very shortly began to take her leave lest some careless, hasty comment should have the temerity to fall from her lips.

As they left Miss Bingley at the front door, Elizabeth expressed the hope that she would come and dine with them: "unless you think the Cobb Hamlet altogether too remote. I believe you may travel in a sedan-chair—I am quite sure that donkeys must be accepted as being far too dangerous."

Miss Bingley merely smiled at this, giving a little bow of assent; and Elizabeth departed, feeling much encouraged by the fact that, not only had her invitation not been given, but it had also not been accepted.

As they turned out of Monmouth Street into Coombe Street, Elizabeth said, rather quietly: "Can it be possible, my dearest love, that Heaven has sent me here to find a husband for Miss *Bingley*? The thought of her living for ever with my poor sister Jane is too dreadful to consider for a moment. Though I was much entertained by the idea of it being Mrs Hurst who now supports Lady Elliot. I quite expected it would be some man, did not you?"

"I did, certainly, and it may be still. With Lady Elliot it is any port in a storm, I fancy. But who shall we find in Lyme for Miss Bingley? What think you of Mr Elgood? He is already a man of property and will probably acquire much more."

"I fear he is too—broad," she answered, taking her satirical tone from him, "and by no means of a suitable height. A man of property, undoubtedly, and certainly a future Mayor. But no, we must think in rather wider terms than that."

"Well, do not let us make ourselves too unhappy on her behalf. If the worst comes to the worst, you know, she can always marry one of her own footmen."

"And I," said Elizabeth, "should be the first to attend such a wedding."

They talked in this vein all the way home, through The Square and behind the bathing beach.

In the afternoon they walked again on the Cobb, rather more formally attired—for it was still Sunday—than usual. This time it was they who were on the upper level when they passed the elegant couple from the inn on the lower one. Hats were raised and bows exchanged. Elizabeth wondered more than ever who they were, but was particularly pleased to find that, with the variation of the tide, her little beach would now be uncovered in the afternoons.

Tomorrow, she would be able to paddle.

VIII

The next day opened with the appearance of a letter from Catherine, brought in by a triumphant James. He went daily to the Receiving Office, but this was the first letter for the Darcy family which had arrived there. It was given to Elizabeth while she sat alone at breakfast, Mr Darcy having altered his routine, so that he now went riding every morning, whether he was bathing or not.

Catherine's letter was as follows:

My dearest Lizzy will, I hope, be cast into transports of delight when I tell her that I shall be with her this coming Friday. Your letter could not have arrived at a better time. My dearest William is obliged to take his ship—*Alcmene* in case you had forgotten—into Portsmouth for a total refit and he will have to be with her most of the time overseeing the work. It is long overdue, as of course we know, and is to take six months. As William says himself, paint will cover damage but cannot repair it. So he proposes to bring me, and Frances and Esther our nurserymaid, to Lyme on Friday and put us off there to stay with you. I hope three will not be too many? We can share a bedroom if it is. I long to see you and your children. William will stay in Portsmouth with his mother. I think I did not tell you that his father was killed last year when a barrel of ale fell off a passing cart and did for him immediately. He does not seem much regretted by anyone and her family have now purchased a charming villa in Southsea for Mrs Price, where she lives with her youngest daughter. My poor sister Susan still awaits her Lieutenant—now a Commander—though he is at last thought to be due at any moment at Plymouth. I pray only that he may be still the person that he was when he went away. Enough of this. My dearest William informs me that we shall sail very early on Friday morning with the rising tide and so you may expect to see us, under full sail, around ten or eleven

o'clock. We shall be the *first* ashore as William means to have the longboat lowered for us! With my love, by dearest Lizzy,
  Your very devoted Catherine.

If this letter did not quite cast Elizabeth into transports of delight, it certainly gave her a great deal of pleasure. After breakfast she went, with Hannah, to see to the accommodation in the second house and was pleased to find that it had a nurserymaid's bedroom which she had not noticed before. The room in which Catherine and Frances, now rather more than two years old, were to sleep was a pleasant sun-filled room overlooking the Monmouth Beach. A short discussion decided that they would breakfast there, Mrs Sidford bringing over the dishes from the third house; and Elizabeth, on returning to her own house, wrote a short letter to Lady Alicia and Mrs Frankland, repeating her invitation at Bath, and hoping to see them again, at least within the next two weeks.

As it was a gentleman's bathing day, Elizabeth did not see Mr Darcy, to give him her news, until he came in for nuncheon.

"I am pleased by this, my love," he said, when she had finished, "as she will be company for you. I am sorry to find we shall see so little of Captain Price, who is a man I greatly esteem, but the demands of his profession are not to be ignored. I make no doubt that her arrival in a warship will make a nine days' wonder here at Lyme. Of what rate is the *Alcmene*?"

Elizabeth had to say she did not know, but rather thought it was a frigate.

"I know she carries forty guns," she went on, "which would be too many, you know, for a sloop."

Mr Darcy smiled admiringly at her.

"How very knowledgeable you are, to be sure, but we must be rather careful here in Lyme, where they do indeed know the difference between one kind of craft and another. I will certainly take my cue from the *other* person."

They went, that afternoon, to the little beach in the Y of the Cobb, alone with their children. Rebecca and Jemima, still declining to enter the sea even up to their ankles, were given the afternoon off and they went together to explore the other part of the town.

As they arrived at the beach, which Elizabeth was much inclined to think of as *their* beach, the last of the tide drained away, leaving it clean and smooth. Their shoes were soon off, their skirts and pantaloons tucked up, and the Darcy family ventured into the sea in a body.

They stood silent for some time, enjoying the contrast between the hot sun on their backs and the cold water lapping at their feet. Then they began to move around a little, avoiding the stones and on the look-out for crabs. The outgoing tide withdrew even further and Elizabeth was quite confirmed in her own opinion, which was that this was the pleasantest beach in the world; and she hoped they would continue to be alone on it.

When they had tired of paddling, Mr Darcy discovered a short plank of wood washed up on the shore, and busied himself with making a castle in the sand, in which he was enthusiastically assisted by his children, though no other plank could be found. Elizabeth selected a dry rock to sit on and was able to view this charming scene with simple enjoyment. The castle did not long survive, its purpose being to be climbed up and jumped off, but the repairs to it proved quite as pleasurable as its destruction. They just took a little longer.

When this was given up, and the children went off again, Alexander between his sisters, to put their feet into the water, Mr Darcy came over and sat on another rather lower rock. He smiled at her as he approached and Elizabeth had to admit that she had rarely ever seen him look so happy.

"I was just amusing myself," she said to him as he, trying for a comfortable position, sat down, "by imagining what Mr Darcy of Pemberley would say to Mr Darcy of Lyme, should they ever happen to meet."

He smiled up at her again and said, after a moment: "I think he would congratulate him, very sincerely, on being a most fortunate fellow. An agreeable house, a beautiful wife, delightful children—I defy even Miss Bingley herself to produce anything one tenth as charming—and the knowledge that there is nothing in the day that requires his attention, beyond the riding of his horse, the eating of his meals and the sleeping of the night through. In short, he is as close to being a free agent as it is possible to be in this world. Any small unpleasantness is to be resolved by some other person—Patton, for instance, or Mr Elgood himself—so that he is in every way a being to be profoundly envied by all who come in contact with him."

"And what would Mr Darcy of Lyme say in reply, do you think?" asked Elizabeth, rather pleased with this little speech.

"Mr Darcy of Lyme would, of course, hesitate to put himself forward before such an august personage as Mr Darcy of Pemberley. But, when he found the courage to do so, he would certainly advise him to take every advantage of his present situation and to lose no opportunity of enjoying himself as much as possible."

He took her hand and said, very softly: "And what has Mrs Darcy of Pemberley to say to Mr Darcy of Lyme?"

Elizabeth smiled back at him and said, not quite so softly: "She has to say that while, as Mrs Darcy of Pemberley, she is incontestably the happiest woman in the world, she is by no means averse to slipping off on a second honeymoon with Mr Darcy of Lyme. Indeed, she would very much like it to become an annual event."

"Then, my very dearest Elizabeth," he said, raising her hand to his lips, "we must see what can be done about that."

They were now aware that they were being regarded, with some interest, by the elegant couple who had dined, on their first evening, at the inn. Elizabeth smiled at them, and waved, and, to her great delight, they smiled and waved back; but they did not join them. They continued their walk to the end of the lower Cobb and then ascended to the upper level. By the time they did so, Elizabeth was once more up to her ankles in the sea and did not see them pass.

"But I am sure," she said to Mr Darcy, as they tried to shake the sand off their feet before putting their shoes on, "that they *would* have come had we suggested it. There are not many houses in the Cobb Hamlet where they could be staying, but I did not think they were *sleeping* at the inn when we saw them first."

The next few days passed smoothly. A rhythm was established. They bathed, they walked, they went on trumped-up errands to the town. The domestic arrangements continued in a settled calm. Mrs Maltby no longer went to the market herself, and she and Mrs Sidford appeared to be on the best of terms. Mrs Wicken delivered a quantity of goat's milk every day, together with an invitation to come and see her "little pretties" whenever they should be passing. The children increased in health and spirits every day. The footmen, the nurserymaids, Hannah, even Patton, grew every day more smiling. In short, they all put on a new bloom which was surprising as, with the exception of the children and perhaps Elizabeth herself, they had all seemed perfectly healthy before.

Elizabeth had to fight off a feeling of gratitude to the scarlet fever that had been the reason for their removal to Lyme. She did not see Miss Bingley again. Her sister Catherine, not seen since her marriage, would arrive on Friday; and the weather continued to be fine, and rather warm.

IX

When Mr Darcy returned to the house, after his morning ride on Friday, he was able to tell Elizabeth that he fancied he had seen a sail just coming over the horizon, from his vantage point at the top of the New Road. His horses were never asked to descend that steep slope. He walked up to meet them on the Sidmouth Road and rode along it, and in the woods and fields towards Seaton.

His information precipitated a certain feeling of pleasurable haste. They hurried over breakfast. Mr Darcy now shared Elizabeth's, between his ride and bathing in the sea, whether his turn or hers. They hurried over their dressing and they hurried along to the end of the Cobb, where the elegant couple from the inn were found to be before them. The man was looking out to sea through a telescope and they were just in time to hear him say: "*Alcmene*, no doubt, my dear. I can see her name. What strange creatures their Lordships at the Admiralty must be, to saddle a perfectly seaworthy frigate with such a name. What does *Alcmene* mean?"

As there was no reply to this, and as they were by now more than just within earshot, Mr Darcy replied, in his gravest voice: "I fancy, Sir, that *Alcmene* was mother to Hercules."

"Then," said his wife, as they must suppose her to be, "she is aptly named. No doubt poor Captain Price has already been required to perform more than twelve impossible tasks by their Lordships."

She turned to Elizabeth.

"We had the intelligence this morning that Captain Price, a former Lieutenant with my husband, was bringing his wife to Lyme today by sea, where she is to spend some time with her sister."

46

"And as I am that sister," said Elizabeth, smiling with deep happiness at the prospect of meeting them at last, "I hope we may now make each other's acquaintance. Our name is Darcy and we are staying in Mr Elgood's houses."

"And ours is Wentworth," said the lady. "My husband is Admiral Wentworth, a former Captain of Captain Price's. They were principally involved, together, in removing the French party from St Helena."

"Then," said Elizabeth, "I believe we have some other friends in common—Lady Alicia and Mrs Frankland. I wrote to them on Monday to ask for the pleasure of their company here at Lyme, and expect to hear, at any moment, of their imminent arrival."

There was perhaps a momentary hesitation on Mrs Wentworth's side before she said: "Then, indeed, I know exactly who you are, how you live in a most beautiful house in Derbyshire, have a charming, pretty sister—who, I must hope, is about to arrive—and, most interesting of all, I think, a very remarkable father."

"Indeed, yes," said Elizabeth, smiling, "I must certainly plead guilty upon all counts. Lady Alicia and Mrs Frankland were observers of my sister's courtship in Bath and were kind enough to say many handsome things about Captain Price. I can only regret that we do not see more of them."

Elizabeth now brought her children forward to introduce them to Mrs Wentworth. They curtseyed very prettily to her and Alexander executed an unmistakable bow.

"That is my name, too," said Mrs Wentworth to Anne, "and I must say that I think it a very good one."

The gentlemen were seen to be conversing amicably together, although the Admiral appeared to be doing all the talking, Mr Darcy merely "taking his cue", as Elizabeth irreverently thought. She was afflicted with a slight sense of embarrassment, knowing so much about Mrs Wentworth's family without her being aware of it, even to the extent of knowing precisely where her divorced stepmother was now living, a thing she probably did not know herself; but she said only: "It is very comfortable being able to make acquaintance in this way. It is one of the great charms of Lyme, I rather believe, that cool formality does not long survive in its narrow streets and gentle sea breezes."

For the first time, Mrs Wentworth smiled at her and Elizabeth found herself thinking what a particularly pleasant face she had. If Elizabeth and her sisters, with perhaps the exception of Mary, were accustomed to being acknowledged as beauties wherever they went, Mrs Wentworth fitted into the even rarer, and more interesting, category of the unacknowledged beauty. Her dark eyes were especially expressive and Elizabeth felt she would like to know her better. She smiled back.

"Yes, indeed," said Mrs Wentworth. "Sometimes one quite tires of being Lady of the Manor, or Captain of the Ship. We have bought a little house here at Lyme, and here we come from time to time, to be nobody but ourselves."

"I have been occasionally puzzled," said Elizabeth, "to decide where in the Cobb Hamlet you might be staying. And, so far, I have come to no conclusion."

"As well you might not," returned Mrs Wentworth, still smiling. "It is a very small house, quite next to the inn where we first saw you; but it holds some particular memories for me. I am more than fortunate in being able to keep those memories unchanged in that house. Perhaps, one day, when I know you better—because I feel we are destined to know one another a great deal better—I will tell you the whole. You are, I am sure, the kind of person who would enjoy a romantic tale."

"Indeed, I should hope so," said Elizabeth at once. "I can hardly imagine anyone being otherwise."

Their attention was now called for by the Admiral, who had been detailing every aspect of the ship's arrival to Mr Darcy. The topsails were already furled—"reefed in," said the Admiral—and they could see sailors far up in the rigging. *Alcmene*, a beautiful sight no matter how much she might be in need of a refit, seemed to glide to a halt not far from where they were watching.

"Foresail," said the Admiral, "mainsail, crossjack. Everything as it should be." He turned to his wife. "I hope the good people of Lyme are watching this demonstration of perfect seamanship, my dear. Captain Price is quite the man we always thought him. But, bless me, what is happening now? Can they be lowering the longboat?"

"My sister," said Elizabeth, rather diffidently, "said she would come ashore in the longboat. And that they would certainly be first."

"Quite so," said the Admiral. "If my wife had ever had courage to set foot in one of my ships while afloat, I should certainly have sent her ashore in the longboat. But, my friends, if they are lowering the longboat we must make haste, or they will be there before us. I fancy," he said to his wife, "that they will beach just below our house."

His words were the signal for a general exodus. The children had been standing on the steps leading to the upper Cobb. Alexander was scooped up by James, without too much protest, and he and the little girls, with Rebecca and Jemima, went ahead of the party, running along the lower Cobb. Elizabeth found herself, with Mr Darcy's hand under her arm, being propelled along at a pace that was faster than a walk but was not yet quite a run. They remained just a few paces ahead of the Admiral and his wife and arrived at the beach, considerably out of breath, just as the longboat was driven upon it.

"Did you see," said Elizabeth as soon as she could speak, "that Catherine was already *in* that boat before it was lowered into the sea?"

"I did not, but if it was so you may be quite sure that it was by no means as dangerous as you thought."

"Well, I should hope not indeed. What if they had been upset into the water?"

"Of one thing I think you may be quite certain. No naval captain of any kind could survive the disgrace should such a thing occur under his command. He would be obliged to walk his own plank."

49

"But how beautiful Catherine has become," said Elizabeth, in surprise. "Had you ever thought she could be so pretty?"

"Your sisters, my dearest Elizabeth, are fixed in my mind as a perpetual source of astonishment and wonderment, not to be outdone on any suit. I had not thought, indeed, that she could ever be so pretty but now that I observe that she *is*, I believe our best course is to acknowledge our relationship to as many people as possible."

They were by the side of the boat when Catherine stepped on to the beach, and she and Elizabeth greeted each other with delight.

"Dearest Kitty, how *well* you look."

"Dearest Lizzy, how *long* it has been."

Captain Price now joined his wife. Her baggage was brought to land, to disappear into the charge of the footman John. Her daughter Frances was safely conveyed from ship to shore and the little party walked up the beach to where the Admiral and Mrs Wentworth awaited them.

A salute passed between the Admiral and the Captain, and a very kind kiss between Catherine and Mrs Wentworth, who then turned to Elizabeth and said: "We have arranged some small refreshment for Captain and Mrs Price at the inn, as I understand that the Captain is anxious to be off in a hurry to take advantage of the outgoing tide. May I hope that you will join us?"

"Nothing could give us greater pleasure," said Elizabeth. "But we, in our turn, have arranged a nuncheon for our travellers at home. May I hope that *you* will join *us*?"

"Nothing could give us greater pleasure," said Mrs Wentworth. "*After* we have been to the inn."

Elizabeth was standing next to Captain Price at this moment, and she was suddenly aware that they were the centre of attention to a large and varied crowd of people assembled on the beach and on the road behind it. As he was looking towards them, Elizabeth was amazed to see him suddenly raise his hat and offer a little bow to someone at a distance. By the time she had turned to see who it was, the person had vanished into the crowd. Elizabeth was inclined to think that it was a woman in a sunbonnet, walking beside a sedan chair; but as she *was* wearing a sunbonnet, which concealed her face entirely, she had no idea who it could be. Captain Price, however, very soon enlightened her.

"Miss Crawford, I fancy," he said, "Miss Mary Crawford of Mansfield. I never forget, you know, that it is to her brother that I owe my first promotion. I did not know she was at Lyme."

Elizabeth could only murmur that she had not known it either.

"It is some time," went on Captain Price, "since I had news of that family. I suppose you could have none yourself? I believe Mr Darcy has a sister at Mansfield?"

"He has," said Elizabeth, "but the other connection seems to be quite broken. I *do* have news of the Crawfords, however, though none of it is very happy. I suppose you could not be mistaken?"

"I could be, of course," said Captain Price, with his charming smile, "but in this case I was not. She recognised me, too. I hope that was not why she turned away so quickly. Also, she has a way of walking, as you may have noticed yourself, which proclaims her to be herself and no one else. I remember it well."

As they went together towards the inn, Elizabeth told him what she had recently learned of the Crawfords from Lady Alicia and Mrs Frankland. He listened attentively, saying only "I am extremely sorry to hear it" or "I hope this is not really the case" at intervals. By the time she had finished her recital they were at the door of the inn, and he turned to her and said: "So if, by chance, I am correct and Miss Crawford is concealed somewhere here at Lyme, I can think of no one more suitable than yourself to find her and bring her back to life. What she must have suffered I can hardly bear to consider, but she could scarcely resist your attentions, I think, or indeed those of my dear Catherine, who would remember her from Bath, were you to offer them to her. I daresay she may be easily discovered. I believe the town of Lyme to be quite small."

Elizabeth merely smiled and disclaimed. She was solely occupied with her own thought on the subject, which was that it was extremely unwise to make foolish jokes at dinner parties. Not only had Miss Bingley turned up in Lyme, but now Miss Crawford was thought to be there as well.

The refreshments at the inn were not very elaborate. An excellent lemonade was offered to the ladies and home-brewed ale to the gentlemen. Tankards of the latter were taken out to the crew of the longboat.

Their whole party moved out on to a little terrace where a fine view of the proceedings attaching to *Alcmene* was to be had. Some members of the crew of the ship were coming on shore, on leave while the refit was carried out, and they were arriving in a variety of small boats all landing on the beach. Captain Price indicated that he did indeed intend to sail with the outgoing tide, due to turn a little after noon; so that he had hardly arrived before he was starting to set off again.

An affectionate farewell took place between him and his wife.

"I leave you in the finest of hands, dearest Catherine, not only those of our dear sister Elizabeth but also those of Admiral and Mrs Wentworth. I shall hope to be able to send for you within the month, by which time I trust my mother's house will be ready to receive and welcome you. I am glad to have the opportunity of attending to it all myself, as my mother is not always very quick to get things done. But I shall not ask you to come until you can be quite comfortable there."

He took his leave of the rest of the party, which now moved up on to the road behind the bathing beach to view his departure. The longboat was pushed out to sea by several interested onlookers from the beach, fishermen and boatmen and one crew member from *Alcmene*, now on leave. When the boat was completely water-borne, Captain Price turned and raised his hat to them, an action which provoked a general cheer and a scattered round of applause.

"Your William has undoubtedly a way with him," said Elizabeth, smilingly to Catherine. "How glad I am to see you both so happy."

With the longboat out of sight, round the corner of the Cobb, they all moved up the hill towards Mr Elgood's houses, from where there was an unrivalled view of *Alcmene*'s departure.

As the longboat was hauled aboard, the sails began to be unfurled and, within a very short time, she sailed serenely away, as magnificent a sight as had ever graced the waters of Lyme Bay.

X

Presiding over her nuncheon table, as she found herself doing some thirty minutes later, Elizabeth was obliged to acknowledge firstly, the immense culinary skills of Mrs Maltby, and, secondly, the organising abilities of Patton. Not one word had she said on the subject of her invitation to Admiral and Mrs Wentworth to anyone other than themselves, but here was the most elegant and succulent repast set before them as though it had been bespoken several days beforehand.

The Admiral did particular justice to all the dishes and his enjoyment was especially reflected in the warmth of his farewell and the fervour with which he carried Elizabeth's hand to his lips. This was by no means unnoticed by his wife who said, with a lurking smile as she made her adieus: "One might think, my dear Mrs Darcy, that my poor husband had never before encountered a square meal, but this, I do most earnestly assure you, is by no means the case. We eat at the inn while we are here and, though their meals are quite excellent, they are *plain*! We have so enjoyed our visit. May I hope that, when next you are passing our house, for I see you go by almost every day, you will knock on the door and come in? I should like it above all things, more especially because, as I now realise, we have a large acquaintance in common."

Elizabeth gave her promise, though she could not be certain when she would be able to do this; but Mrs Wentworth continued: "Tomorrow is your bathing day, I think, and after that it is Sunday. But let us take every advantage of the indigenous informalities of Lyme and allow me to say that, whenever it is convenient to you to call, you will certainly find me at home."

It was not yet two o'clock. Their little beach would be under water for another two hours, but it was Mr Darcy who proposed, particularly to Catherine with the hope that her momentous journey had not tired her, to accept the invitation of Mrs Wicken, the goatherd, to go and see her "little pretties".

The suggestion was eagerly taken up by Jane and Anne. Elizabeth and Catherine made no objection and they shortly set out, with one footman carrying Alexander and the other carrying Frances, and all three nurserymaids, for the path that led to Seaton, over the Ware Cleeves.

It was an afternoon of singular beauty. The sun shone through slow clouds, lazily moving from the south-west. The bees murmured among meadows already cut for hay, and butterflies hovered everywhere. There were innumerable scents in the air and a blanket of peace seemed to have been laid upon them. There was not another soul to be seen.

They went over a field into a wood. Emerging from that, they found themselves in another field which went down to the edge of the cliff. Below them the Cobb could be seen, anchored, like some great reptile, in the sea; and far, far beyond there was a full-rigged ship which might still have been *Alcmene*.

A little further on, a young man was to be found, sitting on a tree-trunk, whittling a stick with a penknife. He had rather the appearance of a footman, Elizabeth thought, though he was by no means in livery. As their own footmen were not in livery either, she clung to her first opinion. He stood up as they passed and wished them a good afternoon, a greeting which they returned. Then, turning a corner in the field, round a kind of knoll in the middle of it, they came upon a lady seated on a stool, her easel set up before her, all the paraphernalia of an artist around her.

She was as startled by their appearance as they had been by hers. She turned to face them as they passed and there could no longer be any doubt. Captain Price had been quite right. It was Miss Crawford.

Mr Darcy and Catherine and Elizabeth, who were all quite well acquainted with her, paused in their walk and Miss Crawford rose somewhat uncertainly as they did so.

"I see that you have found me out," she said, with some attempt at cheerfulness, "but I beg you will *not* demand to see the products of my labours. I am a very indifferent artist."

There was a chorus of words in which "delight", "pleasure" and "charmed" seemed to predominate and then a sudden silence fell, which Miss Crawford filled by saying: "It is a perfect afternoon for a long walk. I cannot conceive where you can be going along this path, but you must not let me detain you."

Elizabeth, bearing in mind Captain Price's words, and summoning all her best courage, replied: "But, dear Miss Crawford, I most particularly wish to be detained. The others are to pay a visit to the goatherd who supplies our milk. I hope I may be allowed to pass the time of day with you, while they go on and do so?"

Faced with such a direct demand for her company, Miss Crawford could only capitulate. With a very good grace and a small inclination of the head, she said: "Indeed you may. It would make me very happy."

"I will await you here," said Elizabeth to Mr Darcy, with a smile. "I must hope Miss Crawford's patience will last at least as long as that."

The departure of the main party left another silence behind it and, on Elizabeth's side, a feeling of some constraint. There was another tree-trunk conveniently placed and on this she sat, quite near to Miss Crawford herself but out of sight of the painting on her easel. At last Miss Crawford said: "I am suffering, and in a contrary way am not displeased to be suffering, from a feeling of some shame. I have been aware of your presence in Lyme ever since you came here. I have even known where you were lodging but could not quite bring myself to call."

Then, after a slight pause: "If I were to be quite honest, and to consult my most truthful feelings, I would have to admit that this was because I was uncertain of my welcome."

"But, my dear Miss Crawford," said Elizabeth, at once amazed by such a confession and disappointed that the warmth of her hospitality could ever be cast into doubt, "we should be delighted to see you at any time, and under any circumstances. You may rest quite assured of that."

"I see that I should have done so," said Miss Crawford, "and it is partly that that induces this feeling of shame. It would have been quite easy for you to have passed by on the other side."

"I hope you mean to explain this to me," said Elizabeth, unable to control a slight edge in her voice. "I would like to think myself incapable of such impoliteness."

Miss Crawford turned to face her more directly.

"But can it be, my dear Mrs Darcy, that the events at Everingham in the spring of last year are unknown to you?"

Elizabeth paused, to gather her strength.

"The fact that your brother died in mysterious circumstances is known to me," she said, as kindly as possible. "Lady Alicia and Mrs Frankland informed me of this when we saw them in Bath two weeks ago. What they did not explain to me was how you were personally involved in the event itself, if indeed this chances to be the case."

"Oh, it was so dreadful," said Miss Crawford, pressing a handkerchief to her lips. "I feel I can never forget it and that everyone is blaming me."

"That I am sure they are not," said Elizabeth at once. "I do not recall that the incident was reported in the London papers. I believe you may be refining too much upon the event."

"You cannot be aware of all the circumstances which went before it."

And silence, once more, fell between them.

Elizabeth could think of nothing to say. There seemed a prohibition on every subject but the one under discussion. At the same time, she was inclined to feel that it was now up to Miss Crawford to relate those unfortunate circumstances or to dismiss the subject completely. She sat quietly, determined to take her cue from Miss Crawford, as Mr Darcy had done with the Admiral.

But it was a very long time before Miss Crawford recollected herself. Then she said, in a much stronger and more cheerful voice: "I beg your pardon, my dear Mrs Darcy—or, indeed, I am sure I could say my dear Elizabeth, for that is how I think of you—for being so silent and uncandid. The truth, which I recite to myself almost every day, is very simple. My brother blew his head off in his own gun room while cleaning one of his newer fowling pieces. It was never established, indeed it never could be established, whether this were deliberate or an accident. That he was almost completely inebriated at the time is beyond dispute. His affairs, when they came to be examined, were in perfect order. His love—I have to name some names— for Fanny Price was a thing of the distant past. Both his loves, in point of fact, made excellent matches—though his face when he heard of Maria Bertram's marriage to your father is something I think I shall never forget—and he could, in any event, have had his pick of half-a-dozen Norfolk beauties had he chosen to lift a finger. What haunts me is simply this. There was no *reason* for him to end his life. If he did indeed choose to do so it was because he did not *wish* to live—and that, as his sister, is a thing that touches me very nearly. It could only mean that Mrs Grant and I, in our capacity as his sisters, had failed in our attempt to give him some further reason for living."

"Indeed, indeed," said Elizabeth, hardly able to contain herself until Miss Crawford had finished speaking, "you must not blame yourselves. I am not acquainted—I am more than happy to remain unacquainted—with the ultimate effects of liquor on the human brain—but this I will tell you. Mr Darcy will not visit his own gun room, alone or accompanied, except in the morning before one drop of wine has passed his lips. But what had the coroner to say?"

"It was brought in Accidental Death."

"Then let us be content that it was that. No blame could possibly attach to you. Indeed, I am sure that, had you chosen to unburden yourself to almost anyone, they would have given you that assurance."

"I discussed it only with the Rector of Everingham."

"And he, I daresay, gave you no comfort whatever. For reasons that I will not go into, at present, I am a little displeased with *all* vicars and rectors and bishops. While you keep along the prescribed path, they will smile and come with you; but should you stray, and fall into the pit full of fire, they will certainly not launch any attempt to rescue you from it."

For a moment Miss Crawford said nothing. Then, suddenly, briefly, she laughed, the amused laugh that Elizabeth remembered from their meetings in Bath.

"But surely you do not believe," she said very soon, "that *I* have fallen into the pit full of fire?"

"Into the Slough of Despond, I prefer to think," said Elizabeth, with a smile. "I believe I was right when I said you refined upon the event too much. If anyone in Lyme outside our immediate circle has ever heard of Everingham I am willing to be amazed; and if one person in a hundred in this charming little town has ever heard of Norfolk, I shall own myself completely surprised."

Miss Crawford did not speak, only smiling at Elizabeth in a bemused way, as though this aspect of the case had not previously occurred to her.

"Why *did* you come to Lyme?" Elizabeth asked directly.

"Oh, we are hiding, make no mistake about that. But it has been a happy choice. My sister's pains eased almost immediately we arrived, and now, between hot sea baths and the sea itself, bathed in and sometimes drunk, and a constant succession of excellent fish dinners, she is in better health than I remember her for a long time. I have left her today in the baths below your house. I will not say she has quarrelled with Mr Davie of Davie's Baths, because my sister does not quarrel. Merely, she has decided upon a change of scene. I think the soft air has much to do with it, too."

"Did you spend the winter here?"

"We did. A darker, damper, more dismal little place than Lyme in the winter is impossible to imagine. Perhaps it suited my mood a little too exactly. But Everingham is most advantageously let. My sister's house in Westminster is most advantageously let. The interest from the money left by my uncle and my most lamented aunt comes thundering into my account on every quarter day. We live in obscurity and some discomfort only from cowardice and, perhaps—since I have listened to your comments with the greatest attention—from a total misunderstanding of our situation."

"Then," said Elizabeth, "let this be the last day of your winter at Lyme. We have a magnificent summer. I have been here for less than two weeks and am entirely enchanted. My children, on whose behalf we came here, grow stronger every day, for they have been down with the scarlet fever as I have not had time to tell you. It is time, Miss Crawford—or rather Mary; I am most happy to drop all formality here—to begin a new life and I, and Mr Darcy and my sister Catherine, and Lady Alicia and Mrs Frankland, whom we expect within a fortnight, will be more than delighted to assist you."

"Then," said Miss Crawford, "I must yield and without *any* reluctance. I am more than fortunate to be surrounded by such friends and it would be churlish not to make the effort you suggest."

"And now," said Elizabeth, rising from her tree-trunk, "I hope we are good friends enough for you to show me what you are painting."

Miss Crawford did not speak, but removed the sheet of paper which had been covering her work. It was the drawing of a wild flower, executed in the greatest detail but still waiting to be coloured.

"It is the Sheep's Bit Scabious," she said. "I have been looking for it for some time. I am so completely set up in my own conceit, you know, that when I encounter a flower I have never seen before I conclude it to be a great rarity, and commit it immediately to paper. I had been looking for it on the cliffs towards Charmouth, but could not find it there. Indeed, the flowers over here are all quite different and I think I must come here again."

Elizabeth praised the clarity of the drawing in all sincerity and said she much looked forward to seeing the finished article.

"I am *not* a landscape painter," said Miss Crawford. "My attempts to paint the Church Cliffs, for instance, ended in the fire. We had some adventures in the early days. I expect you saw my faithful Robert as you came along. We heard of amazing things, like the Spittles and Cain's Folly, and thought they must be worthy of a painter's brush. But there is a kind of gorse which grows between Lyme and Charmouth, which has longer, sharper spines and fiercer, denser bushes than any other kind of gorse and so we gave up on our quest. Also it was supposed to be the haunt of smugglers. But as for the Black Ven, when Robert eventually found it, it was nothing but a take-in."

"The Black Ven!" said Elizabeth, in awe-struck tones.

"Yes, *indeed*. I, who had been brought up with Mrs Radcliffe, had visions of a dark chasm in the cliffs, with a ruined castle or two upon the top and a kind of oubliette arrangement—for the unwary traveller, you know—underneath. But, however, it turned out to be nothing of the kind—a part of the beach, only to be seen at extremely low tide and very slippery at that. Even Robert has never managed to walk across it, but he assures me it is quite unsuitable as the subject of a painting."

Here, it seemed to Elizabeth, was the old Miss Crawford and they conversed on a number of light-hearted topics until Miss Crawford said she had to rescue her sister, "or she will be permanently pickled, I imagine, in brine like an onion."

They contrived to leave a note for Mr Darcy, pinned to the tree-trunk. They summoned Robert, who packed up the artist's materials very neatly and with great despatch, and then they set off comfortably together, down the hill towards the town.

XI

Mr Darcy was an intolerable time arriving. Miss Crawford had declined to come in and had set off at once to rescue her sister. Waving her on her way, Elizabeth was aware of an overpowering need to discuss the afternoon's events, and the time passed very slowly. Some tea was brought in by Patton, who said, as he put it down: "I hope I may venture to ask, madam, if there is something amiss?"

"There is nothing amiss, my good friend," said Elizabeth. "Certainly there is no deceiving you. I am a little overset by an encounter this afternoon. I hope your tea may put me right. But do, pray, tell Mr Darcy, if he should ever return, where I am to be found."

The tea calmed her and to such an extent that she was able to smile at Mr Darcy when he came, some ten minutes later, rather anxiously into the room.

"What *can* Miss Crawford have said to you, my love, to put you all on end? You have managed to disturb the undisturbable Patton."

"Well, I am sorry to have done that and no doubt, when I came in, I looked even wilder than usual. But the only thing Miss Crawford said—and I *must* start to think of her as Mary— to upset me was that her brother blew his head off in his own gun room and the verdict was brought in as Accidental Death."

"Ah," said Mr Darcy, wisely. "You mean our encounter at Tunbridge Wells."

"I do mean that but I do not mean to mention it—except, of course, to you. One does not, you know, jump off *cliffs* by accident. I believe there are no cliffs in Norfolk, so he could not, as it were, have had any practice, no experience, as you might say, of cliffs. Which, one must assume, was why he chose those not very high ones with a good sandy landing place at the bottom."

Mr Darcy took her hands and smiled.

"You are right, I am sure—and it is also very kind in you to be so concerned. You are perhaps merely suffering from an attack of your own good nature. But I think we are condemned to silence on that head. An accident in a gun room is by no means uncommon, whatever we may privately think. Was Miss Crawford still very troubled by it? It cannot be very recent."

"About a year, I think. Shortly after our visit to Tunbridge Wells. She seems to think that everyone here has heard about it and she remains covered in shame."

"Well, what I think is this. It can be no service to Miss Crawford even to hint that her brother might have attempted, once before, to take his own life. Let her believe in the Accidental Death. We must take a little vow of silence there."

"And we shall also never be able to ask whether or not she saw us that time in the Dipper's Hall."

"That, perhaps, is a matter of more moment," said Mr Darcy, smiling again, "a question without an answer. Let us agree between us that she did *not* see us and that he did *not* know who we were. We have already consigned Mr Crawford to that other place, with Lady Lucas and Mrs Norris, although they have yet to arrive there. I think that must be punishment enough."

"It is quite strange to me that he should ever have thought Fanny Price, as she then was, likely to respond to his overtures. Now that I have met her."

"I rather imagine he assumed that he had only to turn and smile at her and she would fall at his feet. Very handsome selfish men—and I fancy that no one had ever said 'no' to him before—tend to inhabit a world of their own there. I think it may be our—pleasure, I hope, privilege certainly—to help Miss Crawford forget him."

"William Price did say something of the sort to me. 'To find her and bring her back to life' were his words."

"Well, my love, we have found her. Let us see how we can proceed from here."

So it was with this in mind that Elizabeth went the next morning to call on Miss Crawford. It was her bathing day but, as both Catherine and Esther, her nurserymaid, proposed going in to the sea, she could easily persuade herself that there was not enough room for so many people in the bathing machine. Abandoning her whole party to the care of Mrs Tegg, therefore, she went on quietly by herself.

"You may ask for Mr Pyne's house," had said Miss Crawford. "You will find it through an archway in the Shambles."

Threading her way between the numerous stalls—the market busier than usual, being Saturday—she had no difficulty in discovering the archway. She paused before going through it. Asking the flower-seller seated by it if this were indeed the way to Mr Pyne's house, she was smilingly assured that it was. She bought a bunch of Sweet-William and Clove-Pinks from her and very shortly found herself lifting the knocker on the door of Mr Pyne's house.

She was admitted, by a maid, into a tiny hall, and was immediately shown into a small sitting-room, which had an uninterrupted view of the sea. Here Mrs Grant was seated, alone, her embroidery on her lap.

She rose as Elizabeth entered and surprised her by giving her a kiss as they shook hands.

"I cannot tell you how overjoyed I was to have Mary's news of your encounter yesterday," she said. "I have sometimes been quite in despair of bringing her out of her glooms, but now that we have met again I hope we may all be able to despatch them on their way."

"I am sure I hope so, too," said Elizabeth. "From what you say, I fear they may be of no recent date?"

"They have been with her ever since we came to Lyme, in fact. While I have benefited in almost every way, she has only sunk deeper into dissatisfaction and despondence. But do, pray, be seated."

Elizabeth sat down opposite to Mrs Grant. She had given her flowers to the maid and they were now brought in, installed in all the grandeur of a glass jug.

"I could not resist them," said Elizabeth. "The flower-seller by your archway had such an engaging smile. And I must remember to get some more for my sister, whose own Sweet-William she is unlikely to see for some time."

"They are charming," said Mrs Grant. "That was the kindest thought."

When the door closed behind the maid, Elizabeth said immediately: "It is such a pleasure to see you move so easily, Mrs Grant. When last I saw you, you were being carried upstairs to our party in Bath."

"Well, yes, indeed, and I can hardly believe it myself. From the very first day here I began to improve. While our excellent cook, a local lady who seems to be related to every person in the town, assures me it is the result of all the fish she gives us, I am more inclined to believe it is owing to the mild climate and my daily immersion in warm sea water."

"Whatever the reason," said Elizabeth, smiling, "no one could be otherwise than delighted by the result."

"You are kind to say so," said Mrs Grant, "and it is a great treat for me to be able to embroider again. My hands were becoming very useless."

She put her work away as she spoke and turned to face Elizabeth.

"It is a great luxury to have you to myself, Mrs Darcy. Mary was so pleased with the different kinds of flower she found yesterday that she is gone there again today—I daresay she will not be back before dinner. So I am able to disclose some innermost feelings to you."

"Then," said Elizabeth at once, "pray do so. Miss Crawford interested us greatly when we knew her in Bath. Mr Darcy and I have wondered, more than once, how she was faring."

"In every material way she has prospered, but in every other way her life seems to be quite without purpose. I wish with all my heart that I could do more for her, but we are so different, for all we were born of the same mother. My own father, whom I scarcely remember, was a gentle, scholarly man. My mother thought he would have become a bishop had he lived. But Mr

Crawford—her second husband—was someone else indeed. He would go his own way no matter how much my mother pleaded. In a sense, he caused her early death, for there was never a moment's peace with him; and, in the end, he rushed one fence too many, at Newmarket."

She paused. Elizabeth, unable to think of anything to say, remained silent.

"I do not mean, of course," went on Mrs Grant, "that Mary is as restless as her father. Some calm, some talent for tranquillity, she must have received from my mother. We live, in truth, very comfortably together; but I am aware, indeed for most of the time, that there is an emptiness, an unspoken regret, within her which I, at least, seem unable to touch."

"She told me yesterday how she still blamed herself for her brother's death. Though one may well wonder how she could have prevented that."

"But what, I imagine, she did not tell you was that it was she who found him first."

"No," said Elizabeth, distressed. "She did not."

"She heard the shot and ran to the place."

"To witness a scene that must remain with her all her life."

After a moment, Elizabeth said: "Forgive me, but while I understand completely why you came to Lyme, is it not the case that there is not enough to occupy her here? You are thrown together a great deal—perhaps too much upon your own resources?"

"You are right, you are right," said Mrs Grant at once. "We fled. We *fled*. Indeed we did, from hostile Norfolk and indifferent London. Now we pay the penalty for finding the obscurity we sought so eagerly at first. Small town life no more suits Mary than did her life in the country, with me at Mansfield."

"And yet, I think, she cannot have been too unhappy there. It is such a delightful place."

"That, undoubtedly. And there she and her brother met a kind of people they had never encountered before—and fell in love, I am sure. But I cannot think a marriage between Mary and Mr Edmund Bertram would have lasted very long and

Maria proved as headstrong as Henry himself. The reverberations of their time together at Everingham still linger. I am only too thankful that we were not there."

Then, after a very small silence: "I hope she is happy with your father?"

Elizabeth did not immediately reply , collecting all her wits.

"Let us say, firstly, that *he* is very happy with *her*. The last five years of my mother's life must have been, for him, a time of great trial. Now Maria is the source of an entirely new life. She has given him two sons and has let the sunlight into his house at Longbourn. On her side, I fancy, there must be something of gratitude. He has taken her from her retreat in the Derbyshire hills and restored her to the dignity of a married woman. They are received in most houses in their neighbourhood, though not, of course, at Court. When one considers the antics of the present court, however, this cannot be regarded as a loss. I do not know how they would get on in London, were they ever to go there. She is become, to all appearances, a contented wife and mother in a rather small society, but whether this is enough for someone who was clearly raised to lead Society, in its larger sense, I fear I am unable to say."

"The birth of your brothers coincided almost completely with the death of Mr Henry Crawford."

Elizabeth could say nothing.

"It was announced in the Gazette on one day and the accident happened the day after."

"But he could not—" said Elizabeth, "she could not—."

Then, taking a deep breath, she said: "She could not have been more lost to him by her marriage to my father than she was on the day she left him. He could not, Mr Crawford could not, have imagined that she would one day return to him?"

"There is no saying, indeed, what he could have imagined. The inner workings of any man's mind must always remain a mystery to me. But there is something very *final* about becoming the mother of twins."

Elizabeth smiled, in spite of herself.

"Perhaps you are right—indeed I am certain that you are. But if Miss Crawford is blaming herself for having failed to give her brother a new purpose in life, and if you are castigating yourself for having introduced him to Maria Bertram, you must allow me to disabuse you both. No blame can belong to either of you. Mr Henry Crawford, as I understand it, was always the master of his own actions."

Then, as Mrs Grant said nothing, she went on: "We cannot alter the past, after all. We can, perhaps, a little influence the future. There comes a time in everyone's life if not to forgive, at least to forget."

Elizabeth was suddenly aware that the tears were pouring down Mrs Grant's cheeks, despite her efforts to stem the flow with a large linen handkerchief.

"My dear Mrs Grant," she said, concerned, "if there is something I have said—."

"No, no, indeed," replied Mrs Grant. "It is just that what you have said has lifted such a weight from my heart."

For a long moment, there was silence in the room. Mrs Grant wiped her eyes and Elizabeth wondered what to say next; but it was Mrs Grant who spoke first.

"I believe what you have said to be true," she said, very calmly. "And I further believe that the comfort you now give me could have been had from other sources, had we chosen to consult them. But I am glad to have received it from *you*. In Bath, you know, we felt we could always depend upon your kindness and excellent sense—and that, let me tell you, is also the opinion of Lady Alicia and Mrs Frankland."

"Then," said Elizabeth, overjoyed if not overcome, "you must do me the honour to believe me. I cannot endure to think that your lives are being blighted by a series of events over which you can have had no control."

In the silence which followed, Mrs Grant regained her composure and Elizabeth recollected the original purpose of her visit.

"I need no invitation, you know," she said at last, "to include you and Miss Crawford in our doings at Lyme. We are come here originally for our health and now stay principally for our own happiness. We have only a few people to offer to your acquaintance. My sister Catherine you already know. Some neighbours of ours, Admiral and Mrs Wentworth, already known to my sister—and a Miss Bingley, sister-in-law to one of my other sisters. I do not fancy that she and Miss Crawford will deal very comfortably together, but that is a risk we must take. If you continue to visit the baths at our end of the town, you could come up to us immediately? We have taken to dining at six."

Elizabeth's visit did not last long after this invitation was given and accepted. She realised, as she left the house, that she was trembling very slightly, but did not forget to buy the nosegay for Catherine. She bought, in fact, the remainder of the flower-seller's stock, the three remaining bunches of Sweet-William and Clove-Pink. She buried her nose in these and, after a very little while, began to feel much calmer; but she was glad to be alone on her return journey.

XII

Much to Elizabeth's surprise, Catherine awaited her at home, completely dressed after her morning's bathe. She must have been with Mrs Grant longer than she had thought.

"The Admiral, my dearest Lizzy, is sent for to London. Their Lordships are in some magnificent fuss which cannot be resolved without him. Mrs Wentworth stopped me as I went past her house, on my way back from bathing, and invited you and me to visit her for nuncheon, should we not be otherwise engaged."

"I think you are acquainted with Mrs Wentworth rather more intimately than you have told me."

"Perhaps I am. She was at Torbay for six months after Frances was born and she came quite often to our house. I grew to like her extremely. And the Admiral's kindness—or perhaps I should say, Captain Wentworth's kindness—to my dear William, when he was only a Lieutenant, is something that William can never forget."

"Then I must suppose that we are *not* otherwise engaged? Is Mr Darcy returned from his ride? I think he will not grudge me to my sister. And Mrs Wentworth is a lady I should like to know *much* better."

She went upstairs very briefly to find another bonnet and to assure herself that *all* her children had come back safely from their morning bathe. She found only peace and tranquillity in the nursery, their nuncheon being almost at an end.

"We had a very good bathe, Mama," said Jane. "Aunt Catherine is up to all the tricks, and this afternoon we are going on a visit to Captain D'Arcy Engineer. Alexander has some shells to give him."

"I am delighted to hear it, my love. Your Aunt Catherine and I are going to call on Mrs Wentworth, but perhaps we may be back before you leave."

Then, arm-in-arm, she went down the hill with Catherine.

They were received at the door, which opened directly on to the street, by Mrs Wentworth herself.

"I hoped you would *both* come," she said, smiling. "But I thought, when you passed just now, Mrs Darcy, that you looked a little *pensive*."

"I am sure I was, a little," returned Elizabeth. "I had been to call on someone we had not seen for some time—indeed, not since Bath three years ago. Some parts of her history—of *their* history, I should say—had left me feeling rather thoughtful."

"Then I ask no questions," said Mrs Wentworth. "You do me a great favour to be here. I do not think the Admiral and I have ever been parted while we stayed at Lyme. Certainly he left for London in no very amiable humour, and I am glad not to be one of their Lordships; but I could not dine alone at the inn, either now or in the evening."

"You must dine with us this evening," said Elizabeth immediately, "and every other evening that you are alone."

"Or you must dine with me at the inn. One of the greatest charms of Lyme is that it is so small. It would give me more pleasure than you can imagine to give a dinner party—shall we say?—on every *other* night?"

Elizabeth and Catherine were side by side on a small sofa. There was only one chair in the room, on which Mrs Wentworth was sitting herself. As she finished speaking, they turned to each other and smiled.

"How charming you look, seated there," observed Mrs Wentworth. "And how very like sisters. I quite envied the harmony between you as I saw you coming along. I never found such a thing with either of my sisters."

"I am sure we sometimes disliked one another very much when we were growing up," said Catherine, somewhat to Elizabeth's surprise. "But now that we are all married and living at a distance, one can only regret that we meet so seldom."

"I also meet my sisters very seldom," said Mrs Wentworth, "but it is by no means a matter of regret with me."

Fortunately—as it seemed to Elizabeth that this remark could not be followed—the manservant now entered, with various dishes that had been brought over from the inn. A table which had stood, folded, by the wall was put up between them and they shortly found themselves, still sitting on the sofa, with all manner of good things spread out before them. The manservant filled their glasses with lemonade—the same, Elizabeth hoped, as they had had yesterday at the inn—and then withdrew.

"We are not *quite* alone," said Mrs Wentworth. "But, even in this tiny house, one maid and one manservant do not constitute a crowd."

"I believe you promised me a romantic tale whenever I should visit you," said Elizabeth, after a moment and trying not to sound too eager. "I hope you mean to tell it to me now?"

"Oh yes," said Catherine. "A romantic tale in what I must call a most romantic house. It makes Mr Elgood's houses seem quite enormous."

Mrs Wentworth was clearly very pleased.

"Well," she said, "you must help yourselves while I am talking; and I will begin by saying, as of course I should, once upon a time."

She drew a deep breath and said, quite slowly: "Once upon a time there was a rather diffident girl who lived in a large house in Somerset. She could play the pianoforte, she could sew very well, she could at least *read* both French and Italian and she knew the names of all the plants in her father's garden. She was, if not precisely *addicted* to poetry, at least extremely fond of reading it and she had read, from cover to cover, many of the books in her father's library."

"I begin to like this lady very much," said Elizabeth. "In this last respect, at least, she is quite like a cousin of my husband's; but she, I think, read only the novels."

"Perhaps that was wise of her," said Mrs Wentworth, smiling, "if only to preserve her peace of mind. But *my* heroine read some of the philosophy and much of the history. She knew, indeed, almost every detail of the Battle of Sedgemoor, which had happened not far from where she lived. She had two sisters and a father, what might be called a godmother in the village, but with none of these people did she really feel at ease. Then, into her life, at the age of nineteen, came a young naval officer, tall, handsome and courageous, afraid of no one but, in the phrase of the day, with only himself to recommend him. They fell in love, of course. He listened to her playing, asked her to read to him and, most telling sign of all, he tried to remember the names of some of the plants in the garden."

Elizabeth and Catherine both laughed at this.

"In a naval officer that is a sign indeed," said Catherine. "I am sure my dear William has no idea which of my plants I have planted and which have come of their own accord—but, because he loves me, I think, he tells me they are all very pretty."

"Then," said Mrs Wentworth, "you have certainly no cause to complain. My Admiral is inclined to admire only what I think of as weeds."

"But pray continue, Mrs Wentworth," said Elizabeth, anxiously. "I hope the romance is still to come?"

"It is, indeed. It is. But not yet, for some time. They agreed to marry, but she—I think it was really she—was persuaded, by the pride of her father and the more reasoned objections of the person I will call her godmother, to abandon the project. She— broke the engagement. He left that part of the country, went back to the sea and she—withered. No," said Mrs Wentworth, in a cooler, more reminiscent voice, "she *faded*."

"But this is so sad," said Catherine. "You promised us a romance."

"Well, I will keep my promise now," said Mrs Wentworth. "Eight years later, through a set of most extraordinary circumstances, based principally on the folly and extravagance of my heroine's father, they met again. He was by now a Captain, rich enough, and to her eye at least, handsomer than ever. They were thrown together, were often in the same company and the only comfort that she had was the knowledge that no one in their party could possibly have known what had happened those eight long years ago. They came to Lyme, on an expedition of pleasure, and one of them, a beautiful young woman only too frequently by the Captain's side, had a bad fall on the Cobb. She was brought into this house, where a friend of the Captain's was staying, into this room—and it was in this room that my heroine overheard the Captain, who was still, I do not need to tell you, the great love of her life, speaking of her in such terms that she began to hope again."

"Oh, I am so glad," said Catherine. "I had begun to feel quite cold."

"So, after a few more anxious weeks, came the happy ending, more remarkable perhaps for the fact that, in general, gentlemen do not ask a second time. But he did so. She accepted. Her father smiled, her elder sister—still unwed—only *looked* her displeasure. They married and he bought an estate in Wiltshire."

Elizabeth was suddenly conscious of a fellow feeling here.

"That relieves my mind completely," she said. "The agony of wondering if a second proposal could be made is not a thing to be forgotten."

"My dearest Lizzy!" exclaimed Catherine. "How can *you* possibly know that?"

"But the *romance*," said Mrs Wentworth, "has yet to be disclosed. The Captain, as you will imagine, was frequently at sea; and so, on one occasion, my heroine came to Lyme, alone, determined, above everything else, to buy this house. She found it in excellent repair, but closed, and empty, and not for sale. She asked here, she asked there, but no one could tell her the name of the owner. Until at last—and this destroys the romance a little, I do confess—she went to the Town Clerk, who informed her—after a suitable hesitation, you know—that it already belonged to her husband."

"Oh, but how charming," said Elizabeth. "A *true* romance, indeed. I was afraid at one point that there would *not* be a happy ending."

"He had bought it," said Mrs Wentworth, with her happiest smile, "within three months of their marriage."

"As a token of his true love," said Catherine. "I find that very beautiful, especially as we can guess who your heroine is. I quite envy you the occasion that you have, to come here whenever you like."

"It is in danger," said Mrs Wentworth, "of growing into an obsession. Since I am opening my heart to the two of you, I will admit that I come here every year in the hope of conceiving a son."

"An old lady of my acquaintance at Torbay," remarked Catherine, "tells me the secret is to eat a great quantity of lobster."

"Lobster!" exclaimed Mrs Wentworth. "Now where, on *this* coast, are we to find a great quantity of lobster? One should never disregard old wives' tales. Unless, of course, she was in the business of selling lobster?"

"Oh no," said Catherine, smiling, "quite the contrary. She grew herbs and kept bees and made mead."

"Then I think we may trust her opinion. So here is some buttered crab, my dear Catherine, and some delicious prawns, which we have every day. But lobsters are another matter."

"Mrs Maltby has spoken to me of rock lobster," observed Elizabeth. "They are not quite the same, I believe, in that they have no claws. Do you think they would serve the purpose?"

"If they have no claws," said Mrs Wentworth, "I fear it would only be daughters."

"To own the truth," said Catherine, "I do not at all know. We have real lobsters sometimes at Torbay, and I have certainly eaten several dozen—but so far without *that* result."

"Nevertheless—" said Mrs Wentworth.

"Nevertheless," said Elizabeth, "I will put it around, through Mrs Maltby, or Mrs Tegg, perhaps—yes, that will be the thing to do—that three beautiful ladies have developed a passion for lobster and a fruitful source will certainly be discovered. And," she said, helping herself to some of the buttered crab, "let them all think what they like."

They laughed at this and Mrs Wentworth said, after a moment, to Elizabeth: "It is just as comfortable being with you as I expected. I thought, when I saw you up to your ankles in the Pool, that there was a person I would certainly like to know."

"I did not know it was called the Pool," said Elizabeth. "We call it Captain D'Arcy's beach, after Captain D'Arcy Engineer, you know, whose name is on the plaque above."

"I had not noticed that," said Mrs Wentworth.

"It was my daughter Jane who discovered him. He has become a great friend of the children—in fact, I rather think they visit him every day—a wonderful excuse for a good walk. So I, too, am quite fond of him."

"I have never brought my daughters to Lyme," remarked Mrs Wentworth. "Where the sea is concerned they are their mother's children rather than their father's. I have always been afraid they would find nothing to do."

"But you are a good sailor, Mrs Wentworth," said Catherine. "When you were at Torbay two summers ago we were often rowed out together to the Admiral's flagship."

"But only in the *calmest* weather," said Mrs Wentworth. "I am without doubt a dreadful sailor. On the one occasion that I sailed, very early in our marriage, from Portsmouth to Plymouth, I was so unwell that I had to be carried to the shore. My poor husband was convinced that I was going to die, as, indeed, I was myself. So I have only visited his various ships when they were docked—or safely at anchor in Torbay."

"Have you left your daughters at home?" asked Elizabeth.

"Most certainly not," said Mrs Wentworth in an amiable voice. "They are gone to one of their godmothers—they have another quite close by—an old and valued friend, a Mrs Smith, at Cheltenham. She lives near the Montpellier Spa, which she visits every day, and they go shopping, and for walks and to concerts in the park, and sometimes even to the theatre, and have hot chocolate at the pastrycook's, and in general lead a life of such dissipation that I begin to wonder if they will ever wish to come home. But I think it right to introduce them to the life of a town quite early. I lived very retired in my young life. When I went first to Bath at the age of fourteen my senses were quite paralysed by the noise."

The table was cleared and the tea brought in. They sat in luxurious silence over this before deciding that they, too, would walk upon the Cobb. As they reached the bottom of the New Road, they could see the Darcy party, including Mr Darcy himself, on its way down the hill; and waited for them. Their walk took on a certain air of festivity, the children at their happiest and Mr Darcy at his most smiling. Their delight was mirrored in Elizabeth's, but she had also a secret satisfaction. She was congratulating herself on her great good luck in having made the acquaintance, so quickly and so easily, of such a friend as Mrs Wentworth promised to be.

XIII

Mrs Wentworth dined with them that evening and joined them as they passed her house on their way to church the next morning.

Elizabeth found herself wondering, as they climbed the steps from Church Street, if Miss Bingley would be there again and how she would respond to an introduction to Mrs Wentworth. Under the circumstances this would be, as Elizabeth regretfully admitted to herself, unavoidable; but she had enough dependence on Mrs Wentworth's strength of mind to be certain that she, at least, would not be at all discomposed by it.

In the event, Miss Bingley did not arrive until they had begun the *Te Deum*. Her pew had been jealously guarded for her by a verger, and she occupied it alone, looking neither to right nor left as she entered. She wore a large straw hat whose provenance absorbed Elizabeth's conjectures throughout the sermon. The text this week, in view of the early harvest, was: "Whatsoever a man soweth, that shall he also reap". Could she have got it in Leghorn? Elizabeth looked about her, as well as she could, for Miss Crawford, but the brim of her bonnet compelled her to look only straight ahead and she did not like to move her head too obviously.

Miss Bingley's occupation of the Monmouth House pew presumably gave her the privilege of walking down the aisle first at the end of the service, because that is what she did, smiling graciously as she passed them. The gracious smile had not faded when she was to be found waiting for them outside, and Elizabeth at once asked Mrs Wentworth if she might present their friend Miss Bingley to her. Receiving a pleasant permission, she did so, mentioning "Mrs Admiral Wentworth" and going on immediately to say: "My sister Catherine, Mrs Price, you of course remember from Netherfield days."

If Miss Bingley was displeased, or disconcerted, by this second introduction, she hid it very well. A certain sharpening of her gaze might indicate that she was asking herself how so many of the portionless Miss Bennets had contrived to find husbands before she had done so herself; but it vanished almost before it had arrived. She inclined her head slightly too kindly towards Catherine and then, smiling again, turned to Mrs Wentworth.

"I hope you will do me the honour," she said to her, "of accepting some refreshment before you embark on your long walk home? If, indeed, as I must suppose, you are the guest of Mr and Mrs Darcy."

"With pleasure, Miss Bingley, and thank you," said Mrs Wentworth. "But I am their neighbour rather than their guest. I live in a small house in the Cobb Hamlet and am only too happy to do so. I much prefer to be outside the bustle of the main town."

"Then you will allow me to lead the way," said Miss Bingley.

She took Mr Darcy's arm as she spoke and they set off, Elizabeth and Catherine following with Mrs Wentworth. Elizabeth used the few moments available to her to explain that Miss Bingley's brother was married to their eldest sister Jane and that they had, before any of them had married, been quite well acquainted with her.

Mrs Wentworth merely listened attentively, only remarking that she knew nothing of Hertfordshire but that she believed it to be very beautiful. Walking quite closely behind Mr Darcy and Miss Bingley they had a clear view of them, and Mrs Wentworth said, in a low voice as they neared the house: "Miss Bingley does not wear her heart upon her sleeve, but her hand on Mr Darcy's sleeve is curiously eloquent. I rather think I understand the situation."

They were no sooner settled in Miss Bingley's sitting-room than refreshments were brought in, indicating to Elizabeth at least that their visit had been anticipated. The cakes, she presently observed to herself, were even more delicious than last week; but, as the compliments and exclamations of delight began to dwindle, a silence promised to fall. To avoid this, Elizabeth said, very clearly and to Mrs Wentworth: "Miss Bingley and her sister had the good fortune to avoid our last winter in England. They were able to spend it in Northern Italy."

"How I envy that, indeed," said Mrs Wentworth. "I do not imagine that I shall ever go there, but the country described at the *end* of *Childe Harold's Pilgrimage* certainly makes one wish to visit it. Did you go to Florence and to Rome?"

"No, we were not so adventurous," replied Miss Bingley, without apparent regret. "We took ship to Gibraltar and sailed from there to Leghorn, where we found a charming villa."

"And I admire that, too," said Mrs Wentworth. "I think I could not endure so long at sea."

"I am sure you were wise to remain at Leghorn," observed Mr Darcy. "There is a certain unrest in the surrounding country-side, and there is a very strong English connection at Leghorn."

"There is," said Miss Bingley, "much to our surprise and advantage. My sister was quite astonished to discover that the façade of the cathedral had been designed by an Englishman called Inigo Jones."

"Is there some recent news from Mrs Hurst and her new companion?" asked Elizabeth.

"Her new companion?" echoed Miss Bingley. "Oh, Lady Elliot, I suppose you mean. But no, there is no recent news."

"Lady Elliot!" exclaimed Mrs Wentworth, before Miss Bingley had finished speaking. "Can this be the Lady Elliot who is, I must suppose, perfectly well known to us all?"

Her question brought about a silence, but Miss Bingley swiftly filled it.

"We met her at the English Legation, where she was in some temporary difficulty," she said, rather stiffly. "An accident, or a defection, on the part of her travelling companion had left her in some trouble. How exactly it was that she came to live with us in my sister's villa I never was perfectly clear."

"And the name of her travelling companion was, perhaps, a Colonel Tilney?" pursued Mrs Wentworth. "I should, in many ways, be glad to be told that it was."

"I believe that was his name," said Miss Bingley, the tone of her voice quite flat. "We did not get a glimpse of him."

Her remark sent a little wave of interest around the room. Mrs Wentworth put down her glass and said, very seriously: "Then I think you must warn your sister, Miss Bingley. Lady Elliot is the divorced wife of my father, whose second wife she was. In that capacity she gave him three sons, for which we must be sufficiently grateful, since it secures my father's title to his own descendants rather than to those of his great-uncle. But he made no provision for her at their separation and she certainly has none of her own. Her stay with your sister is liable to be a very long one, though in one sense I am only too happy. I cannot quite like to think even of her as destitute upon a foreign shore."

"I think—I hope—" said Miss Bingley, "that she is not quite as destitute as you suggest. There are English merchants at Leghorn, though by no means as many as there were, and on more than one occasion she went alone to visit one and returned with large sums of money concealed about her person."

"It is a charming picture," said Mr Darcy, with a smile to Miss Bingley. "May I hope you thought so too?"

"Certainly I was very much relieved," said Miss Bingley, rather reluctantly returning his smile, "to find that she had *some* means of support. My sister is very soft-hearted, but I must confess I did not care for Lady Elliot."

"I understood, when we were at Bath last month, from Lady Alicia herself, perhaps, that Colonel Tilney had returned without his family's jewels," said Elizabeth.

"He could not do so, indeed, as my sister Elizabeth has them all," said Mrs Wentworth, somewhat dryly.

Then recollecting herself, she said: "You must forgive us, Miss Bingley, for all this mysterious cross-talk, but your information is of enormous interest to me. My elder sister Elizabeth married, as his second wife, a General Tilney, father of the Colonel we are discussing, but she was widowed within the year. She then announced her intention of keeping the family jewellery until such time as Colonel Tilney should marry, which now, of course, appears increasingly unlikely."

"He has a brother," said Catherine, who had not spoken before, "who is a clergyman and who has more children than one cares to mention. His wife's brother, also a clergyman, is married to our sister Mary."

Mrs Wentworth laughed, a particularly delightful little laugh.

"It is a web, indeed," she said, "a charming spider's web. But your sister's sister-in-law need not worry. Her jewels are quite safe. My sister will certainly never part with them to anyone else and would, I think, guard them with her life."

There was a small pause in the conversation after this. Miss Bingley herself filled up her guests' glasses, as the servant had withdrawn; and, while she did so, Mr Darcy remarked to Mrs Wentworth that Miss Bingley's sister was a great admirer of the work of Lord Byron.

"Is she so?" said Mrs Wentworth. "I can equal her enthusiasm for the early poems but there is something about what he has written recently that I cannot quite like. Perhaps I am too old-fashioned, more used to sailing in the calmer waters of Grey and Cowper and Wordsworth. He has a tendency now, in my husband's phrase, to sail a little too close to the wind. Though you will observe," she added, with a smile, "that I have read enough of his latest work to be able to say this."

Elizabeth returned her smile.

"Which we must all admire, indeed," she said. "I believe that Mrs Hurst had hoped to meet Lord Byron himself."

"She set out with that intention," said Miss Bingley, "certainly. But no sooner had we landed at Leghorn than he removed himself to Genoa."

"I am sure there was no connection between these two events," remarked Mr Darcy.

"There could not have been," said Miss Bingley, almost sharply, "since we are entirely unknown to Lord Byron."

"But is not Genoa quite close to Leghorn?" asked Catherine.

"By no means as close as we thought," said Miss Bingley, with the kindest smile. "Indeed by road it is in the region of a hundred miles, through very dangerous country. It is usual to make the journey round by water, but only in boats of the country, you know, quite full of vermin and most unsafe. We ventured only as far as Pisa, with a member of the Legation as our escort. The great tower there is in some danger of falling over and we were determined to see it before it did so."

"I hope you do not mean to tell me that you did not see Lord Byron at all," said Elizabeth.

"No, I do not," said Miss Bingley, at once. "He came quite often to Leghorn, where I fancy he had business with his banker. And to collect his letters, so we were informed. He was by no means *persona grata* at the Legation, so there was no question of meeting him there."

"One can only feel," said Mrs Wentworth, "how deeply distressed he must have been by the death of his friend Shelley, whose poetry, I am forced to confess, I infinitely prefer to his. It would certainly add, at the very least, a new shade to his character."

Miss Bingley now transferred her attention to Mr Darcy. Elizabeth very quietly asked Mrs Wentworth if she could dine with them on Wednesday before asking Miss Bingley to do so. Receiving a pleased assent, Elizabeth gave her invitation to Miss Bingley and it was most joyfully accepted. They rose very soon afterwards. Miss Bingley, with great affability, conducted them into the hall.

Elizabeth and Mr Darcy went in front, Mrs Wentworth having indicated that she would like to walk with Catherine.

"We mean to chatter about our summer at Torbay, converse which might not be endurable to any third party, you know, no matter how well disposed," she said pleasantly. "And I think perhaps I am the slowest walker of you all."

XIV

As they turned once again into Coombe Street, Mr Darcy said: "That was a superlative lemonade, Elizabeth. I trust Mrs Maltby may have the receipt?"

"I trust so, too. And the cakes were excellent. They have quite obliterated the tedium of that sermon."

They walked companionably together for some moments, until Mr Darcy said: "You have found a great friend in Mrs Wentworth, I think. I must see what I can do to attach the Admiral. Do you think he might like to ride in the mornings?"

"The Admiral still gives the impression that he is only just becoming used to walking on the ground, as if he were sometimes surprised by its stability; but I am sure he would be delighted to be asked."

They waited by Mrs Wentworth's house for the two others to arrive and parted from her there, having received her smiling reminder that they were to dine with her that evening at the inn.

Elizabeth did not forget that she had to speak to Mrs Tegg about finding a supplier of true lobsters, and she went down with Mr Darcy and Alexander on the Monday morning, talking to her while they changed.

Mrs Tegg was silent for a moment after Elizabeth had finished speaking and then favoured her with an enormous smile.

"I'll speak to Tegg, my lady," she said. "They comes from a distance and sometimes costs more than most folks is willin' to pay. But if you're his customer he needn't have no fear about the payment."

"Mrs Wentworth and I will undertake to buy any he can come by—within reason, of course."

84

"Mrs Wentworth as well?" said Mrs Tegg wisely. "Then I'm sure I'm very pleased for you both. I said to Tegg the other day how well you was both lookin'."

Elizabeth observed Mrs Tegg's covert examination of her person with equanimity, merely telling herself that a constant supply of real lobsters was now quite certain, since nothing could ensure it so completely as a speculation of that sort. She informed Mrs Maltby, who received the information with a smile but no comment; and four enormous lobsters were delivered to the house in the course of the afternoon. Superbly dressed, their appearance at dinner caused a small pause. Silent glances were exchanged by the ladies—for Mrs Wentworth was with them—but it was Mr Darcy who said: "It was, I think, one of our King Henrys who died of a surfeit of lampreys. Knowing nothing of surfeits, and nothing at all about lampreys, I was inclined to feel sorry for him. Now I believe that death from a surfeit of lobster, for instance, might be a thing to be most sincerely recommended. There would be so much pleasure on the way."

His remark was received with some laughter and a pretence of disapproval, but Elizabeth only said: "I wonder, indeed, just how *much* lobster would constitute a surfeit? I am quite willing to try and discover at least the point at which *enough* lobster can be considered as good as a feast."

"I have always thought that a very foolish dictum," said Mr Darcy. "Enough is nothing like as good as a feast. So pray, my dearest Elizabeth, contrive a surfeit of lobster for us all as soon as may be conveniently possible."

"Indeed, my love," said Elizabeth, with her warmest smile, "I shall give the matter my very closest attention."

As the tide was now out in the afternoons, they could go once more to the little beach at the Pool. Mr Darcy had found a carpenter to make wooden spades for the children and one, rather more secretly, for himself. Elizabeth and Catherine sat contentedly together, talking sometimes, but very often companionably silent. They watched the rise and fall of many a castle in the sand and went, from time to time, to cool their ankles in the sea. It was, without question, the most delightful form of idleness and it had also, without any argument at all, the advantage of being immensely beneficial to the health of everyone concerned.

As they came back from one of their visits to the sea, Elizabeth happened to glance up, to find Miss Crawford settled behind them on the lower Cobb, her easel planted before her. She was absorbed in her work, which was being observed by Mrs Wentworth, from her position behind Miss Crawford but on the upper Cobb.

Seeing that she was discovered, Miss Crawford merely placed a finger on her lips and said, quite loudly: "Now do not say a single word, I beseech you, but return to your places exactly as you were before. I believe I may have found a new talent in myself."

Elizabeth and Catherine went back to their previous positions with some assumed docility. After a few minutes, Miss Crawford asked Mr Darcy if he would hold his spade in a particular way for a moment and then she said, in the greatest glee: "Now it is not often—indeed, I rather think it has never happened before—that I allow *anyone* to look at my work before it is finished, but now I absolutely require your total commendation before I venture any further. Here is an undoubted portrait of the Darcy family extremely busy on the beach and I am quite astonished to think that I never thought of doing such a thing before."

Elizabeth and Catherine had no difficulty in admiring the drawing when they arrived, still barefoot, on the Cobb. It was a charming group. Mr Darcy, Jane and Anne were putting the final touches to a handsome, turreted con-struction—"Perhaps a trifle larger than the one they actually made," said Miss Crawford with a smile—Alexander and Frances sat to one side, engaged in some game of their own, while Elizabeth and Catherine occupied much of the foreground, doing nothing at all. There could be no doubt as to the subjects of the drawing and Elizabeth and Catherine both said so immediately.

"Here is the stimulus I have been asking for," said Miss Crawford in high good humour. "The Darcy family must be worth more than several Sheep's Bit Scabiouses—what, I wonder, is the plural of scabious? I hope it is not scabii—or even," in mock solemnity, "a Viper's Bugloss. I had much trouble with that. I could not believe there could be so many flower-heads attached to one stem, and whenever I was sure I had drawn the last one another one appeared. Until, you know, I got quite *angry* with it. But it is my masterpiece so far—I think of having it framed, indeed. But here, before me, and so *suddenly*, is a new life! I must be forever grateful to my subjects."

They were still comfortably engaged in admiring the drawing, and without any dissembling, when Mrs Wentworth came up to them, having successfully made her way down one of the perilous flights of steps from the upper to the lower Cobb. Elizabeth presented Miss Crawford to her at once. A smile, a small bow, were exchanged between them and Mrs Wentworth immediately said: "But I feel I am already well-acquainted with you, dear Miss Crawford, through our friends Lady Alicia and Mrs Frankland. And I am *very* pleased to have a closer look at your drawing. I was just too far away up there."

After a few seconds of close observation, Mrs Wentworth went on: "But you must continue—do not allow us to interrupt you. You should start to colour it at once while the sun is so kindly placed. Though what you will do for water out here on the end of the Cobb—"

"Oh," said Miss Crawford, smiling, "I always travel with my own water, and not the greatest lady in the land can say that, I fancy. One's own sheets, one's own wine, one's own carriage and servants—but I never heard of anyone else travelling with their own water. If we could just attract Robert's attention—"

But Robert, perhaps suspicious of some crisis, already hovered behind them. The water and the paint-box were discovered. Elizabeth and Catherine returned to the beach and Mrs Wentworth found a seat on a rock behind them so that they could enjoy a friendly, disjointed conversation. And there they stayed until the sea began to encroach upon their little beach and Rebecca and Jemima came to collect the children.

"Yes, you may look," said Miss Crawford, to them all, "though I have a long way to go. Especially Mr Darcy, if you please. I am a little disturbed by the angle of his hat."

"I think, Miss Crawford," said Mr Darcy, after a careful examination of the drawing, "that the angle of my hat is not to be improved on, or disputed, or criticised, in any way. It is exactly the angle at which a very happy man, sedulously engaged in a wholly useless occupation, which is nevertheless demanding *all* his skills and intelligence, *would* wear his hat. I must congratulate you on your drawing. You have captured us completely and I think we must be very pleased to be your prisoners."

"Charmingly said, Mr Darcy, and I thank you. I could not wish for greater praise."

Mrs Wentworth now began, with a series of delicately probing questions, to find out if Miss Crawford were engaged to dine anywhere that evening and, shortly discovering that she was not, asked her if she would join them at the inn.

"With all the pleasure in the world, Mrs Wentworth. But I think I am now obliged to inform you of the existence of my sister, who has been spending the afternoon in your local baths. I do not perfectly understand why she has deserted Mr Davie, but desert him for the moment she undoubtedly has."

"Then will she be able to accompany you? I hope there may be no very profound reason for her visit to the baths?"

"She suffered for some time from pain in her joints, a simple arthritis one might suppose. But the medical profession is so anxious to please its patients that one practitioner will say one thing, and another, another, and quite of the same affliction, that there can be no agreement among them. If you wish to have gout, you must go to Doctor X, but if you prefer it to be rheumatism, then you must consult Doctor Y. My sister has been so remarkably free from pain since we arrived at Lyme, however, that we no longer discuss the nature of her malady which is now, I dare to hope, a thing of the past. But in order that it may remain so she does visit the hot sea water baths every day. By which I would be understood to mean, if you can forgive my roundaboutation, that she is recovered from whatever ailed her before and is now engaged in preventing a recurrence."

"Then it can be no inconvenience for her to dine with me," said Mrs Wentworth, "since I hold my dinners at the inn; but my house, which is immediately next door, is just large enough to contain the two of you, and me, before the dinner is quite ready. And there can be no need to change our dress. Let us wisely adopt the manners of this charming place and all be vagabonds together."

"I shall indeed be only too happy," said Miss Crawford with her pleasantest smile, "and my sister too, without a doubt. I would not like to say how long it is since we dined from home."

The dinner passed off very well. Mrs Wentworth attempted an apology to Mr Darcy for confronting him with such a monstrous regiment of women, but Mr Darcy simply said: "John Knox, I think, beyond any question one of the more disagreeable personalities in the history of the world. And if you know of a civilised man who could object to dining alone with five handsome and very agreeable women, I should be most interested to meet him and hear his reasons."

His words were received with general acclamation and the evening passed only too quickly. Elizabeth was delighted to find a dish of lobster as part of the first course and had the greatest difficulty in not catching Catherine's eye while it was on the table before them. It was demolished entirely.

Wednesday brought Miss Bingley to dine with them and she arrived, to Elizabeth's hardly concealed astonishment, on foot, attended only by a manservant.

"I am obliged to eat my words," she said as she entered the room. "It is no distance at all behind the beach and on an evening like this an even longer walk might give the greatest pleasure. I see, too, that you have a most charming view from this room."

Her words set a pattern for the evening. Elizabeth had never seen Miss Bingley so anxious to please—not, that is to say, since she had married Mr Darcy herself—and gave full credit to Mrs Wentworth for having brought about this change. The conversation did not falter and Miss Bingley and Mrs Wentworth left together, a little after nine o'clock, to walk back in what was left of the twilight. Elizabeth could not have believed that a dinner with Miss Bingley at such very close quarters could have been so pleasant.

Friday found Mrs Wentworth dining with them again and, just as they rose to go in to the dining-parlour, the Admiral himself was announced.

"You will forgive me, I hope," said he, addressing Mr Darcy rather than Elizabeth, "for presuming on such a relatively short acquaintance; but, being informed that my wife was to dine with you—I was informed, indeed, that it had become quite a habit—I could not resist the temptation to try if her invitation might not be extended."

He was welcomed simultaneously by all the occupants of the room, delighted to see him again, hoping his journey had not been too arduous and that his mission to London had been successful. It was not, however, until they were seated at table that his wife was able to say to him, with one of her most beautiful smiles: "I am quite charmed to observe, my dear, that you have achieved a complete victory over their Lordships."

"I have indeed," responded the Admiral. "You know me too well for me to be able to conceal it. But, if you allow me—" he said, turning to Mr Darcy, "I should like to give you a toast."

"Most certainly I will allow it," said Mr Darcy, "but you must allow me to provide something rather more worthy of your toast than what we have in our glasses at present."

After a very short conversation with Patton, their glasses, in a very short time indeed—and to Elizabeth's ever-increasing astonishment—were filled with champagne.

The Admiral gave his toast and they all drank "Confusion to their Lordships" with great enthusiasm.

"It is not that I really wish evil of any permanent nature to their Lordships," said the Admiral, "although I must admit in my innermost heart that I do, but conferences with them on the subject of ships which are going to *sea*, containing *sailors*, who are living beings like all the rest of us, involve a degree of frustration which must exhaust the patience of a greater man than I. Every one of them is a political placeman, with no knowledge of sailing, or of seamen, or the sea, and their chances of ever acquiring that knowledge are now being very considerably reduced."

He took another mouthful of champagne and smiled at them all, as though by no means displeased that his listeners remained quite silent.

"The canal in St James's Park," he said, addressing himself particularly to Elizabeth, "as you may not have had occasion to discover, is being transformed into a romantic pond. The work of destruction is already begun so there is no sailing upon *it*. Their Lordships must now be obliged to obtain their nautical experience as far afield as on the Serpentine, since an open sheet of rough water, such as the River Thames at Westminster, though infinitely nearer, must be considered as altogether too dangerous for *them*. *And* it is tidal into the bargain."

They laughed and exclaimed at this and the dinner party increased in amiability until it was almost over. Then, in answer to a question from Mr Darcy, the Admiral replied: "Well, I will not burden you with *all* our deliberations. Suffice it to say that, if their present Lordships had their way, there would not be a single man-o'-war left in the line. They are determined that only merchantmen are now required and cannot be persuaded to understand that merchantmen must be protected from pirates, for instance, and all other ill-disposed craft. While it is true that we are not, just now, at war, it is absurd to suppose that this happy state of affairs will last for ever, as their Lordships enthusiastically imagine."

Then he said, directly to Catherine: "I chose to ask one of them, behind my hand as you might say, if he had any information about *Alcmene* and was astonished to be told, as I did not expect any reply, that the work was proceeding well but that it was to cost more than had been projected. But my amazement lasted only as long as it took me to realise that that answer could be given to almost any question that you might care to think of."

The Admiral, in short, was in excellent spirits. Mrs Wentworth, happy and contented before, took on a new glow in his presence. The evening passed effortlessly in talk and laughter and they parted only at eleven o'clock in the comfortable certainty that they would all be dining together at the inn on the following day.

XV

The Admiral's great good humour was not to last for long. At dinner the next day Mrs Wentworth said, very quietly to Elizabeth: "Our peace is entirely cut up at the prospect of a visit from my sister Elizabeth. She comes next Tuesday to obtain a signature from my husband. He and my sister Mary's husband are to be trustees for my three little half-brothers—the sons of the Lady Elliot now at Leghorn. She has had the good sense—my sister, I mean—to write for rooms at The Three Cups, quite at the other end of the town—as she and my husband can only be in company for five minutes without coming to blows. I speak, of course, metaphorically, but her presence, even at *that* distance, will be like a wasp constantly circling one's head, and always evading one's efforts to execute it."

"I believe," said Elizabeth, equally softly, "that we have had the pleasure of meeting your sister. I am sure that she came to our farewell party when we left Bath on our first visit."

"Then," said Mrs Wentworth, with one of her most charming smiles, "you know exactly what I mean. I hope only that she will go away once she has obtained the signature. But," she went on, very earnestly, "this brings to an end for the moment our comfortable arrangement for dinner. I think it may well be wise to see what effect this visitation will have upon the Admiral."

It was on that same Tuesday that Lady Alicia and Mrs Frankland arrived. Mr Darcy took the carriage to meet them at Axminster, his own coachman driving hired horses.

They came, invested in their own kind of gaiety and good humour, exclaiming at the beauty of the view, the charm of the little houses and their great delight in being once more at the heart of the Darcy family. They bestowed a kiss on both Elizabeth and Catherine, remarked with great pleasure on how well they were looking and in general gave the impression that their visit to Lyme was quite a pinnacle of happiness.

"We have brought only one maid, my dear Elizabeth, as you may see, as we remembered what Mr Darcy had said about the lack of space. And what could equal our astonishment but to discover that they had both *wished* to come. In the end they had to draw lots."

"And Lyme is not in any way like Lisbon," added Mrs Frankland, "although one could pretend that that distant view over the bay is like the one over the Tagus. But in fact it is nothing of the kind. We are already quite converted. We were never very convincing as Weymouth people—and must see if we cannot do better as Lyme people."

They called on Mrs Grant and Miss Crawford the following morning and came back divided between their satisfaction at the improvement in Mrs Grant's health and their disappointment that Miss Crawford should still be looking so sad.

"And we came by the Assembly Rooms," said Mrs Frankland. "Much smaller than we expected, but giving the impression that one should go there to *enjoy* oneself. Do they hold their Assemblies during the summer?"

They were seated at nuncheon when she said this and her question was, for a moment, unanswered. Then Patton cleared his throat and said, to Mr Darcy: "If I might speak, sir?"

"Certainly. Indeed," said Mr Darcy with a smile, especially to Mrs Frankland, "in all matters pertaining to Lyme, Patton is our great intelligencer."

"The Assemblies are held principally on Thursdays at this time of the year," said Patton. "That is to say tomorrow. They begin at five o'clock and the entrance fee is sixpence."

"At five o'clock!" exclaimed Lady Alicia. "And when do they end?"

"I understand, my lady," said Patton, in his gravest voice, "that they have been known to extend until midnight. There are two intervals for supper, one at seven o'clock and the other at half past nine."

"Then," said Lady Alicia, "if I might propose such a thing, we could arrive after the first supper and stay until the end of the second? And I must make it plain, immediately, that this is to be my party. I shall invite the Wentworths as well, but Miss Crawford, I think, is not yet ready for junkets of this sort."

Elizabeth was surprised to find that, though she had never once contemplated a visit to the Assembly Rooms herself, the prospect was a very happy one. What might be regarded as ball dresses—for neither had prepared for such an occasion—were taken out of their closets by Elizabeth and Catherine, to be ironed and made ready to wear.

It was further decided, though Elizabeth was not clear by whom, that the ladies should make the journey in sedan chairs; and a fleet of these was bespoken, from the Cobb Hamlet and from the town.

"Mrs Tegg says you are to go in their sedan chair, Mama," said Jane, as they walked home from their morning bathe. "There are two Mr Teggs, you know, one in front and one behind. They are called Zachariah and Zebediah and only Mrs Tegg knows which is which. I do like Mrs Tegg, Mama, but I wish she had some more front teeth."

Their procession moved off, after a dinner at the Darcys' house, exactly as planned. The Admiral and Mr Darcy walked beside their wives; Lady Alicia and Mrs Frankland had a footman each; and Patton himself accompanied Catherine. The arrival of five sedan chairs at the Assembly Rooms occasioned considerable interest and they were very civilly escorted to the far end of the room, where some tables and chairs stood by themselves, alone, unoccupied.

The room shortly began to fill with people returning from the supper room. They were comfortably engaged in examining them when, to Elizabeth's astonishment, Miss Bingley came into the main Assembly Room, clearly that minute arrived, and by herself.

"I think," said Elizabeth, in a very low voice to Catherine, "that Miss Bingley is indeed come to Lyme to look for a husband. One must be glad that she is now old enough to have no need of a chaperon."

It was not long before Miss Bingley observed them and came over, broadly smiling, to speak to them. Elizabeth had no choice but to present her to Lady Alicia and Mrs Frankland, and to the Admiral, still in London on the previous Sunday. A chair was found for her and it seemed tacitly agreed that she now formed part of their party.

"My housekeeper met your housekeeper this morning at the market," she informed Elizabeth, "so that is how news of your projected visit to this place reached me. I have long wanted to attend one of the balls here but did not quite like to do so alone. I was sure I could depend upon your good nature if I came this evening."

She smiled, not quite triumphantly, at Elizabeth, who now engaged her in conversation with Lady Alicia and Mrs Frankland. They were quite willing to receive her as one of their party, and shortly began to discuss with her the respective merits of Lisbon and Leghorn.

Miss Bingley's appearance had created a little stir among them, but it was presently eclipsed by the arrival of a very upright man, almost too well-dressed for a ball at Lyme. He stood for a moment at the entrance, examining the crowd through an eyeglass. Then he turned, and ushered into the room an equally well-dressed woman. She was wearing a particularly noticeable brooch.

Elizabeth recognised her at once as Mrs General Tilney, remembered only too clearly from their visit to Bath. Mrs Wentworth, after a slight intake of breath, faced Elizabeth and Catherine and said, very quietly: "It is my sister and Mr Elliot, my father's former heir. It is some years since we had any communication with him, or from him, and his presence here is altogether very unfortunate. I cannot imagine where my sister can have found him. I hoped she had already left Lyme."

"His nose was quite put out of joint by the birth of your brothers," said Mrs Frankland, overhearing this. "But, though it is a prominent feature, from this distance the disjointing scarcely shows."

Mrs Wentworth smiled a little but was still, and obviously, very uncomfortable.

"It is quite out of the ordinary to realise that my sister is step-mother to the man who, if report be correct, has recently abandoned *our* step-mother—that is to say the Lady Elliot at Leghorn. The gossip is that he put all the family jewels into her lap and then bade her an instant farewell. But our cousin Elliot is another matter. He came here once before when we were here. What *can* his business be, here at Lyme?"

"Whatever it is," said Catherine, who was facing the door, "we may now be about to discover. You cannot escape, I am afraid. They are upon us."

Mr Elliot was indeed upon them, widely smiling and saying, as soon as he was within earshot: "Lady Alicia—and Mrs Frankland—I could hardly believe my eyes. What an unexpected, undeserved pleasure to find you *here* and apparently in such excellent health and spirits."

Before Lady Alicia could reply, he went on: "And my cousin Anne and the Admiral! And Mr and Mrs Darcy! How charming to be among such a host of delightful friends! I think there is no need at all to present another cousin to you, Mrs General Tilney."

Lady Alicia now rose, smiling not too unconvincingly, and said: "Most certainly there is not—and, in my turn I must present to you Mrs Darcy's sister, Mrs Price," nodding at Catherine, "and her friend Miss Bingley."

Bows, courtesies, were exchanged, but it was shortly obvious to Elizabeth that something about Miss Bingley had attracted the close attention of Mrs Tilney.

She was still reeling from the fact that Mr Elliot knew who she was, but now noticed that Miss Bingley was wearing a large brooch on her bosom; and a momentary glance informed her that it was the pair of one on Mrs Tilney's.

"I hope you mean to tell me," said Mrs Tilney to Miss Bingley, and without any preamble at all, "where you acquired that brooch."

"Certainly," said Miss Bingley, suddenly all smiles. "I acquired it in Italy earlier this year."

"I hope you mean to tell me how that came about."

"I purchased it from a Lady Elliot, whom we had encountered at Leghorn. She was in some embarrassment and I was happy to assist her out of it."

"You must be aware that it is the twin of mine."

"I have been aware of that ever since you entered the room. I understood that Lady Elliot had received it as a gift from a certain Colonel Frederick Tilney."

"Indeed? It is an important part of the Tilney family inheritance—a Florentine brooch of the late sixteenth century."

Miss Bingley paused, but only for a moment.

"I naturally never thought of asking Lady Elliot for a bill of exchange," she said, coldly and angrily. "And if I had, I doubt that I would have brought it with me to a festivity of this kind."

"You misunderstand me, I think."

"I think not," said Miss Bingley, now entirely mistress of the situation. "I gave Lady Elliot an excellent price for her brooch. Only to discover," pausing again to survey her totally captive, and extremely attentive, audience, "when I returned to London—that it was made of paste."

"*Paste!*" said Mrs Tilney, almost aghast. "I declare I had no notion."

"As of course you could not," continued Miss Bingley calmly. "My opinion is that Lady Elliot is in process of having all her jewels copied and may well sell all the copies on. In this way, you know, she may remain comfortably in Italy for the rest of her life."

A chair was now found for Mrs Tilney and she sat down. A breeze seemed to pass out of the room as she did so.

Elizabeth, mesmerised by what had just occurred and still desperately wondering where she could have met Mr Elliot, suddenly noticed the complete change that had come over him as he regarded Miss Bingley. She was assailed by a very beguiling thought.

It was at this moment, fortunately perhaps for the good temper of everyone concerned, that Lady Alicia found herself accosted by the Master of Ceremonies.

"I was most felicitously informed of your ladyship's presence among us," he said, with a smiling glance at Mr Elliot, "and have dared to hope that you would open the dancing for us when we recommence after supper."

"Oh dear," said Lady Alicia, with an unsmiling glance at Mr Elliot, "I really had no intention of dancing. But perhaps your opening caper may not be too energetic. Pray, what is it to be?"

"Hunsdon House, my lady, a country dance—by no means too taxing. I would like to say that we seldom find such distinguished company in our rooms at this time of the year. I hope we may prevail upon you to honour us by leading the way?"

Lady Alicia, the undisputed daughter of an Earl, albeit one in the Peerage of Ireland without visible means of support, had no choice but to agree. The Admiral offered himself as her partner; Mr Darcy requested the pleasure of dancing with Mrs Frankland and the remainder sat quite still to see whom Mr Elliot would select. He was standing just behind Miss Bingley's chair and, after a hesitation only too visible to Elizabeth, he asked her to dance with him. She accepted with the greatest alacrity and the three couples walked off behind the Master of Ceremonies.

XVI

They left behind them a complete silence. Two sisters faced two sisters across a small oak table.

"I have been very rude," said Mrs Tilney.

"Yes," said Mrs Wentworth.

"Who is Miss Bingley?" asked Mrs Tilney.

"She is our eldest sister's sister-in-law," said Mrs Price.

"Where is her husband's estate?" asked Mrs Tilney.

"In Nottinghamshire," said Mrs Darcy.

"And where is that?" asked Mrs Tilney.

"It marches with Derbyshire," said Mrs Darcy, "where my husband has his estates."

"Somewhere in the north, I suppose," said Mrs Tilney.

"You are still being very rude," said Mrs Wentworth.

Four glasses of champagne now appeared, creating a diversion most acceptable to them all. After a few moments, and over an almost empty glass, Mrs Tilney said: "He should have danced with one of us."

"Yes," said Mrs Wentworth, "but I do not ever wish to dance with Mr Elliot. Where did you find him?"

"He is staying at The Three Cups."

"I hope you have obtained the Admiral's signature?"

"I have. But now that I have met Mr Elliot again, I think a third trustee may be no bad thing since he and I are now both widowed."

"My dear Elizabeth," said Mrs Wentworth, almost too astonished to speak. "Consider what you are saying."

"I have already done so. Mr Elliot has every appearance of being a very rich man. I think it desirable that his money remain in the family."

"And do you think you can attach him now?"

"I have every intention of trying."

"He was very unkind to his wife. He treated Mrs Clay abominably. He was unpardonably rude to our father."

"Not, I think, without provocation in all three cases. He is older now. And so am I."

"I cannot wish you to be made unhappy."

"As I said—I am older now. More difficult to wound."

Elizabeth and Catherine were sitting together, actually holding hands. To their great relief, the dance now ended and they were no longer sole witnesses to the sisterly exchanges occurring opposite them.

"I hope," said Catherine to Elizabeth, "that we never arrive *there*."

The evening proceeded without let or hindrance. Lady Alicia declined to dance again. Mr Elliot redeemed himself by partnering Mrs Tilney once, before returning to Miss Bingley. Mr Darcy danced with Catherine and the Admiral with Mrs Frankland. Elizabeth, to her great delight, found herself alone with Lady Alicia and Mrs Wentworth, as Mrs Tilney had walked off.

"So Mr Elliot is married?" asked Elizabeth, deciding that the direct question was the best way to discover what she wished to know.

"He was widowed some years ago," said Mrs Wentworth. "He then set up house with a Mrs Clay, daughter of my father's man of business, but that also came to an end. I understand he gave her the money for a post-chaise and sent her back to her father."

"But how charming of him," said Elizabeth. "Perhaps she was well out of that bargain."

"I think she was," said Mrs Wentworth, "though she was never a favourite of mine. But I also think that Mr Elliot, whose fortune was made by a first marriage, would require an almost equal fortune in a second."

"That he would certainly find in Miss Bingley. Do not you think, Lady Alicia," said Elizabeth, "that they make an ideal couple?"

"Well," said Lady Alicia, not quite laughing, "perhaps I do. And it would certainly prevent misery in two *other* people. But why do you dislike Miss Bingley so much?"

"I do not altogether dislike Miss Bingley," said Elizabeth. "On reflection, there is a small region between liking and disliking—and that is where I place my feelings for Miss Bingley."

"We have only to tell Mr Elliot that Miss Bingley is a personage of large fortune and the matter will be quite settled," said Mrs Wentworth. "Except that we must now recall that my sister Elizabeth has entered the lists."

At this point they were approached by the Master of Ceremonies to request that they would make up a set, adding very kindly that it was the Rows of Barley, and that all the hard work was undertaken by the men. They acquired three bashful young partners and were just getting acquainted with them when they were joined, at the bottom of the set, by a slightly over-dressed couple, not quite in their first youth.

Elizabeth could not see the woman, as she was on her side two or three dancers below her; but her appearance created a considerable disturbance at the top of the set. Mr Elliot, accompanied by Mrs Tilney, left the set and left the Assembly Rooms. Elizabeth managed to catch the eye of Mr Darcy, dancing with Catherine and a long way up the set, but he merely sent her one of his more delightful smiles.

As the dance progressed Mrs Wentworth, who was standing next to her, said in an undertone: "What an evening of amazements, indeed. The woman with the bright hair and pearls is Mrs Clay—Mr Elliot's former mistress. I hope she will not recognise me."

She did not. The dance ended and they all went down to the second supper.

"I have discovered what you wish to know," said the Admiral, coming over to them and with a lurking smile. "Her husband is the Mayor of Taunton and they are regular visitors to Lyme."

"It took me a moment to recognise her," said Mrs Wentworth. "But a great improvement, I think?"

"I never met her," said the Admiral, "but have heard of her, of course. It was Elliot who could not withhold his exclamation."

"I wonder where she got that colour for her hair," said Catherine.

"Your hair, my dearest Catherine," said Elizabeth very sternly, "is a most beautiful colour and it is *not* to be tampered with."

Mr Darcy and the Admiral escorted Miss Bingley to her door, returning to perform the same office for their wives. Their cavalcade of sedan-chairs returned safely to the Cobb Hamlet in the light of a rising moon.

Alone in their bedroom at last, Mr Darcy said, before Elizabeth could speak: "I am even a little before you, I think. I am sure I discern a wedding in your eye. I have told Elliot the exact size of Caroline Bingley's fortune—that is to say, what it originally was. But she is a lady living very little at her own expense and there may well be some augmentation of her principal. I told him that her brother had a respectable estate in Nottinghamshire and that her sister was the widow of a man of whom he had actually heard. Altogether, I am inclined to think that I sent him home with an entirely new light in his eye, although the little skirmish with the former Mrs Clay dimmed it a little. I have to say that there is something about him that I cannot quite like but, putting the happiness of your sister Jane somewhat above that of Miss Bingley herself, I think the match well on its way to be made."

"How *delighted* Jane will be," said Elizabeth. "I must write to her tomorrow."

XVII

The Admiral now rode regularly with Mr Darcy in the mornings. A little reluctance on his part—he felt safer on his own legs than on anyone else's—had been overcome. After two excursions down the Sidmouth Road he was able to compliment Mr Darcy on the excellence of his mount. He had never before ridden such a handsome and biddable beast, he said. It had cured him of thinking one horse to be much like another.

"For which I can only offer my apologies. I know how angry I become when anyone assumes one *ship* to be like another."

The day after the Assembly Ball was a Gentlemen's Day. Having seen the Admiral depart for his dip in the sea, to be followed by a ride to Seaton, Mrs Wentworth paid a morning call upon Elizabeth.

The conversation, instantly started, continued headlong, with everyone frequently talking at once, until Lady Alicia, in a moment of comparative silence, said: "So what it comes down to is this. How happy would we be if a friend of ours were to marry Mr Elliot? And the only one who can give a sensible answer to that must be his cousin Anne."

There was a small silence. Mrs Wentworth, slightly disconcerted by such a direct application, did not speak for a moment. Then, smiling again, she said: "Except that I am not perfectly clear if Elizabeth and Catherine regard Miss Bingley as a friend?"

Once more there was an infinitesimal silence, broken this time by Catherine.

"When first we knew her," she said, "we thought her very old and very proud and she certainly never bestowed more than a glance on us, the younger Miss Bennets. This, I am now quite willing to agree, was entirely our own fault—our behaviour at the time is a thing to be ashamed of. But—if we thought of her at all—it was to sympathise with our sister Jane, whose sister-in-law she was fated to become."

"You did not think of her as having a first interest in Mr Darcy?" asked Mrs Wentworth, still smiling.

"No, indeed we did not," said Catherine, very decidedly. "When Lizzy announced that she was to marry him, we felt nothing but amazement—that is to say *I* felt nothing but amazement because I had never had any reason to think about it before."

"Then I think we may assume," said Mrs Frankland, "that Miss Bingley is *not* a friend."

"Not of an intimate kind, at least," said Elizabeth. "After an acquaintance of nearly ten years we remain Miss Bingley and Mrs Darcy to each other—that is to say, when she remembers. It is very often still Miss Elizabeth. But I should not be happy to see her married to someone whose character is not above reproach."

"Ah," said Lady Alicia. "Here is the nub of the matter. What do you say, my dear Anne?"

"Well," said Mrs Wentworth, "a great deal, I think. His first wife was married only for her money, reported to be in the region of forty thousand pounds. That he was very unkind to her I know from an unimpeachable source and certainly she died relatively young. I do not suggest, you know, that there was any close connection between the two events, but unhappiness can be at the root of much indisposition. Then he was—indeed cruel, I think, is not too strong a word—to a friend of mine," turning to Elizabeth, "my daughters' godmother, in fact, my dear Mrs Smith—whose executor he was. That is to say, he did nothing—he declined to act, reducing her to actual poverty. And finally, having lived with Mrs Clay for a very appreciable time, he sent her home with nothing but the money for her journey."

She paused for a moment, but no one spoke. Then she said: "This is scarcely to describe the behaviour of an amiable man."

"The three women in these cases," said Mrs Frankland coolly, "had one thing in common. They were entirely in his power. Two of them, one must suppose, had status inferior to his, in his own estimation quite certainly. The third appears to have been helpless unless he chose to assist her—which he did not. By this I would be understood to mean that Miss Bingley, as compared with these unfortunate ladies, is by no means at his mercy. Her performance last night, indeed, proves her a lady of spirit and resource, but," she continued, a triumphant glance including them all, "we must nevertheless recommend her to proceed only on the advice of a reputable, reliable, redoubtable—attorney!"

There was laughter at this.

"And have we the courage to do so?" asked Lady Alicia. "Who will bell the cat?"

"I might," said Elizabeth, "if only to smooth the way for my poor sister Jane, whose sister-in-law she will always be. If, that is to say, Miss Bingley would deign to listen to a parcel of provincial nobodies, which is certainly how she regards us."

"What sort of life does Mr Elliot lead in London?" asked Catherine. "I am sure he has no occupation."

"He was bred to the law, as the saying has it," said Mrs Wentworth, "but, if he has eaten his dinners, that is his sole preparation for practice. I believe he has set himself up as a kind of *arbiter elegantiarum*—since Captain Brummell went abroad, you know, that situation has been quite vacant. Which is to say," to Catherine, who was looking a little puzzled, "he tells people how to behave."

"Miss Bingley would certainly assist him there," said Elizabeth.

"But he is constantly at cross-purposes with the patronesses at Almack's, who seem perfectly conversant with all the circumstances of his marriage," said Mrs Wentworth.

They looked expectantly at her.

"Her father was a grazier, I believe in the West Country somewhere, and her grandfather actually a butcher. He was intended for my elder sister Elizabeth," said Mrs Wentworth, in a sudden burst of candour, "and when his wife died we did rather wonder—and now that Elizabeth is a rich widow I had *also* started to wonder, though this is the first time to admit it. But I am now very surprised to find that that same Elizabeth is apparently considering it herself."

"So—can we give this match our blessing?" asked Mrs Frankland. "Or—do we do our possible to prevent it?"

"We do neither," said Lady Alicia, very calmly. "We shall emulate his own behaviour and do nothing. We do not even know why he has come to Lyme. Perhaps there is another wife and family here."

"How very exciting that would be," said Catherine. "How can we possibly find out?"

"I will remember to ask Patton in the morning," said Elizabeth.

They were now interrupted by Mr Darcy and the Admiral, looking particularly pleased and happy after their morning's exercise.

"We have made a most desirable discovery," said Mr Darcy, "on account of the Admiral's having lost his hat to a sudden gust of wind."

"And it was a serviceable hat," went on the Admiral, "indeed a good friend of some year's standing, so we set off to find it. The wind, indeed, behaved in such a way that one might almost believe it was deliberately leading us towards the charming little district that we found—that it was determined to show us the perfect place for a most romantic picnic."

"We found the hat impaled upon a rose bush at one end of a most beautiful green glade," continued Mr Darcy. "Below it the trees sloped down towards the sea, but above it there were little precipices and chasms, crowned with wood, you know, and altogether much like an illustration to the *Mysteries of Udolpho*. But what was strange was to find that the grass was everywhere quite short."

"Goats, my love," said Elizabeth, in her most commonplace voice. "Have you not been trespassing into the kingdom of Mrs Wicken?"

"Well, perhaps we have," said the Admiral. "But we are agreed to hold an exploring party there before the grass gets any longer."

"We shall host it together," said Mr Darcy, "as one should at a picnic, and are come to demand your approval of our scheme. If the weather remains as dry as at present we can take carriages down the whole way. We shall be able to invite Mrs Grant."

A murmur of agreement followed his words.

"But if we are to be hosts, my dear Admiral," said Mrs Wentworth doubtfully, "we can scarcely avoid Mr Elliot—or my sister if she is still here."

"And we can in no way avoid Miss Bingley," said Elizabeth.

"But we had no intention that you should," said the Admiral.

Mr Darcy merely grinned.

"And Miss Crawford, my love?" asked Elizabeth. "How will she deal with Miss Bingley?"

"I think it will be of benefit to us all," said Mr Darcy, after a moment and in his gravest voice, "if their first collision takes place in the open air."

XVIII

Elizabeth received a note from Mrs Wentworth the next morning, saying that, as she had received, from an impeccable source, the news that her sister was to dine with Mr Elliot that evening, she hoped that they would *all* dine with them at the inn.

Everyone was in especially good spirits. If the Admiral and Mr Darcy were a little dashed to be told that their secret discovery was a well-known beauty spot called the Great Glade in Pinhay Woods, they did not let it depress them for long. The innkeeper, who had given them this information, threw himself into their project, promising every assistance.

Mrs Tilney, however, unseen and unencountered, continued to haunt them from afar. The very fact of her presence had completely ended their accustomed tranquillity and Elizabeth longed for her to go.

Visiting Miss Crawford the next day, she and Catherine were greeted with the following words: "I hope *you* may be able to tell me who is this patronising, intrusive woman whom I met on the Cobb yesterday. She stood behind me, looking at my picture—that great unfinished masterpiece, you know—and said: 'If that is the Mr Darcy that I know—and it quite certainly is—I am sure he would never wear such a foolish hat and most particularly not at that angle. What a clown you have made him look.'"

Elizabeth and Catherine almost laughed, but realised that Miss Crawford was quite serious and they did not wish to hurt her.

"We *can* tell you, and we will," said Elizabeth. "But what else did she do?"

"She said: 'But you have got those hills very well,' and walked off before I could reach for my battle-axe."

Now they could laugh and they all did so.

"When one thinks of the trouble you took over that hat, and the permission you received from its wearer, that was a comment of the cruellest kind," said Catherine. "And you must not regard it. That incident shed an entirely new light on my esteemed brother-in-law."

"We did not see her so frequently in Bath, I think?" said Elizabeth to Catherine. "I remember her only at our farewell dinner."

"But your husband," said Catherine. "Once seen, never forgotten."

"You may remember her yourself," said Elizabeth to Miss Crawford. "Mrs General Tilney and the elder sister of our neighbour Mrs Wentworth. As unlike her as possible. We understand—from an impeccable source, of course—that she remains here to woo a certain Mr Elliot, who is a cousin, so that his money may remain in the family."

"A Mr Elliot?" said Miss Crawford. "Do we have a Christian name for him?"

"We do not," said Elizabeth. "That is to say—we have forgotten."

"Nevertheless, I believe him to be an acquaintance. How would Mrs Tilney respond to a little gentle competition?"

"Not well," said Catherine. "Not well at all. And we hope to settle him on our Miss Bingley."

"Is Mr Elliot really so desirable?"

"There are at least two opinions on that point," said Elizabeth. "I believe you have yet to meet Miss Bingley."

"But from *his* point of view," said Catherine, "I think there might be safety in numbers."

"It is a situation," said Miss Crawford, "which gives a certain spice to our unremarkable existence."

Elizabeth now asked after the progress of Miss Crawford's painting.

"I have been back twice to the Cobb to complete the background. Mrs Tilney accosted me on the second occasion. And I think I do remember her—rather too much jewellery and a *very* handsome man who, she pretended, was her stepson?"

"Correct," said Elizabeth. "On both points."

"Then I am sorry that I did not find my battle-axe," said Miss Crawford. "But to continue. I am in general so perfectly satisfied with the results of my labours—which, of course, must mean that I am not an artist at all since no artist is ever content with the final result—that I plan to have my painting framed and hope you will accept it."

"But nothing in the world," said Elizabeth, flattered and delighted, "could please me more. Do you think you can tell me when we may expect to see it?"

"Well, there," said Miss Crawford, "I should be unwise to specify a date, when I think how many things can go irreversibly wrong. But certainly I can commit myself—to the *near* future!"

Elizabeth, now addressing herself to Mrs Grant, then gave her invitation to join their exploring party.

"If the weather should remain like this, you will be able to travel all the way in the carriage, so I hope very much that you will feel able to come."

"Then I must repeat your words, Mrs Darcy," said Mrs Grant. "Nothing in the world could please me more. I can now walk quite well, you know, and indeed did so the other day, all the way back from the Cobb Hamlet. And it has lifted my spirits to an extraordinary extent. Mary, I am sure, will need no persuasion to accept."

"Indeed she will not," said Miss Crawford, "and if it is to be a picnic in the old style, where everyone contributes a little to the feast, I trust that you will allow me to do so. I have a friend in the market who murmured to me this morning that he still had some cherries and now plums approaching a peak of perfection, so I think I will go and bespeak his whole produce for Monday."

"I believe you must have heard of Admiral and Mrs Wentworth," said Elizabeth to Mrs Grant. "She and her sister are the daughters of the Sir Walter Elliot whom you may remember from Bath. They will bring their cousin Mr Elliot and *we* shall invite Miss Bingley, now residing at Monmouth House."

"Is that her name?" almost demanded Mrs Grant. "She is a great *un*friend of our flower-seller in the archway, who says that she drives a very hard bargain."

"There is a general conspiracy," said Catherine, after a moment, "to marry off Miss Bingley to Mr Elliot. You must do nothing to hinder this happy outcome, unless you can discover, from your flower-seller perhaps, that he has a wife and large family already living at Lyme."

"If Miss Bingley has upset our flower-seller, then she deserves a moment or two of discomfort," said Miss Crawford. "I greatly look forward to your party."

Sunday was a day apart. Elizabeth felt obliged to have her hair done properly and to put on the most formal of her day dresses. Mr Darcy submitted to the attentions of Patton for a full half-hour and emerged looking handsomer, and more elegant, than ever.

They met downstairs, by the front door.

"Do we go to church alone?" asked Elizabeth.

"We do, from this house, that is to say. No wage could be large enough to compensate for sitting through another of those sermons. They are all to take a sedate walk to the Ware Cleeves, where they may play at battledore and shuttlecock if no one else is looking."

He took her arm, as they left the house, and said, reflectively: "I sometimes think that this is the true meaning of *noblesse oblige*. Is it, I wonder, too early in the season for the text of the sermon to be 'for of thorns men do not gather figs, nor of a bramble bush gather they grapes'? While I should be but too happy to receive a sermon on this subject from Our Lord Himself, His chosen minister at Lyme has a way of obfuscating every word of every parable so that they end by meaning nothing. But that, my dearest love," he said, with another charming smile, "is *quite* between ourselves."

Catherine awaited them, with Lady Alicia and Mrs Frankland, and the Wentworths joined them as they passed their door. They occupied one pew entirely, the Admiral at one end and Mr Darcy at the other.

Elizabeth was eager to see if Mr Elliot would accompany Miss Bingley to church and they did arrive together; but they sat separately, quite correctly, on opposite sides of the aisle, and did not look at one another during the service.

Mr Darcy was not far wrong. The text of the sermon proved to be "A good tree bringeth not forth corrupt fruit", and he held Elizabeth's hand quite tightly during it, squeezing it slightly every time a comment from the pulpit proved more than usually nonsensical. It appeared that there was a glut of plums in Dorset.

Once again Miss Bingley waited for them outside, Mr Elliot attentive beside her. Mrs Wentworth made her known to the Admiral; Lady Alicia and Mrs Frankland surrounded Mr Elliot and Mr Darcy followed with Elizabeth and Catherine.

"I have to say," said Mr Darcy to Miss Bingley, once more in Monmouth House and in his pleasantest manner, "that only the thought of the refreshment that I hoped you would offer us again supported me through that sermon. We were, in fact, informed before we left Derbyshire that the vicar here was exceptionally long-winded; but the source of our information was not one that could be absolutely trusted."

"I much enjoy being able to invite you in this way," returned Miss Bingley. "I miss my sister every day, but more than ever on occasions where one is required to be both host and hostess."

"I wonder if you have any news from Leghorn this week?" asked Elizabeth.

"Unfortunately not," said Miss Bingley. "Indeed, I begin to be a little alarmed at this considerable silence."

"I trust that there may be nothing amiss," said Elizabeth, as sincerely as she could. "And to take your mind off any such possibility, we have planned an expedition to the Pinhay Woods tomorrow. I hope you will be able to accompany us? We feel it best to take full advantage of this weather while it lasts, so I hope this invitation is not too sudden."

Miss Bingley replied with what was, for her, great cordiality and undertook to be at the Darcys' house at half past ten o'clock the next morning. They were in time to hear the Admiral give a similar invitation to Mr Elliot, who accepted with alacrity and almost too much enthusiasm. Very shortly afterwards, the supply of charming little cakes being totally exhausted, they took their leave and returned to the Cobb Hamlet.

The day ended with an afternoon stroll to the end of the Cobb, and this was followed by a magnificent sunset, offering the promise of a glorious day on the morrow.

XIX

Elizabeth was perfectly happy to hear, from Mr Darcy later that evening, that the Admiral was in charge of all the transport arrangements. Her whole household was invited to their picnic. Mrs Maltby and Mrs Sidford, alone, refused this invitation, looking forward, no doubt, to a day of calm repose while everyone else was at Pinhay.

The day, therefore, began early, with a train of donkeys being loaded with interesting-looking baskets, just below her window.

At half past ten precisely Miss Bingley arrived, attended by a heavily-laden footman.

"You will allow me, I hope, to contribute some of the cakes that my cook makes so well. I was uncertain how many people were invited to your expedition, but I am of opinion that no expedition of any kind could ever be provided with too many cakes."

Elizabeth laughed with her and thanked her, thinking that she had never before seen Miss Bingley so informally dressed and, apparently, so well disposed towards the world in general. They were shortly joined by Mrs Wentworth and all the ladies of the party then quietly climbed the hill to the Sidmouth Road, where the carriages awaited them.

Lady Alicia and Mrs Frankland, with Mrs Wentworth and Miss Bingley, led the way, in the Darcys' own carriage. A hired coach came next, with all the children, Hannah and the nurse-maids; and Elizabeth and Catherine were taken up by Mrs Grant and Miss Crawford, who had hired a carriage from The Three Cups. The gentlemen were all on horseback, each one escorting one of the carriages, and, rather to her surprise, Elizabeth found that they were to be accompanied by Mr Elliot. She made him known to Mrs Grant and Miss Crawford, who said to him immediately—as she was sitting on the side of the carriage next to him: "I believe we once had the happiness of dancing together—at Stornaway House, did we not, Mr Elliot? On the occasion of the ball they gave to honour the birth of their elder son. I recall that it was one of our more dashing dances—a quadrille, perhaps, for old Lady Stornaway would never permit the waltz to be danced even in the seclusion of their own house."

If Mr Elliot was taken aback at the beginning of this speech, Elizabeth thought he had recovered by the end of it.

"Certainly, I attended that ball, Miss Crawford. I remember it as one of the most brilliant occasions of that year—perhaps *five* years ago, would you agree? But—" he looked at her much more closely, "could you be the young lady who lost an earring in the middle of our dance together?"

Miss Crawford laughed, quite loudly, and with real amusement.

"You have placed me precisely, Mr Elliot. I am not certain whether to be complimented or condemned, for between hunting for my earring and getting confused by the demands of the dance—then quite in its infancy, I fancy—we made a great mess of it together."

Mr Elliot seemed unsure whether to laugh or not. He contented himself with an elegant smile.

"I remember that we did not find your earring at the ball," he said. "Did it ever appear afterwards?"

"Oh yes, certainly it did. It had fallen into my bosom, you know, and lodged there quite safely for the whole evening. I found it when I undressed for the night and was excessively pleased to do so, since it was one of a pair that had been my mother's—*our* mother's," she said, turning to Mrs Grant. "But not, I fancy, quite as pleased as Lady Stornaway herself, who had turned her house upside down in pursuit of it and all without result."

"I am charmed to hear it," said Mr Elliot. "I understand that Lord Stornaway has left London and is now resident in Scotland?"

"Do not let us destroy this beautiful day by talking of Lord Stornaway, Mr Elliot, or spoil this delightful occasion. Nothing must be allowed to cast a cloud upon it. *We* are quite strangers to Lyme—that is to say, our residence is of less than a year. Perhaps you know it rather better?"

Their conversation continued in calmer vein, with some help from Mrs Grant and Elizabeth, until they found themselves safely deposited at one end of the Great Glade.

Trestle tables, covered with plain linen, had been put up wherever the shade was deepest, and benches placed round them. At the far end of the glade donkeys, relieved of their loads, could be seen grazing the excellent grass. Finding shade for the carriages was difficult, but patience brought success. The horses were then taken out of their shafts and led away to join the donkeys.

Elizabeth, possessing herself of her daughters, set off with them to the more interesting end of the glade. She found herself unexpectedly joined by Mrs Wentworth.

"Could anywhere be more perfect for our purpose?" asked she. "Truly I think I have never seen such a *convenient* spot for a picnic of this kind—Mother Nature has excelled herself. I believe there is even a stream in the trees at the far end. But I have really come to warn you," she said, lowering her voice a little, "that the Admiral intends to kidnap your Patton, or at least to set the press gang upon him. Not, I must add, for any direct benefit to him, or to me, but it seems that their Lordships at the Admiralty are in need of a new Captain at the Victualling Department and he is convinced that Patton would fill the post to admiration."

"I will warn him, certainly," said Elizabeth, "and I am especially pleased that he should have earned the Admiral's commendation. In fact there is no end to his excellence, or his versatility, and if we were unaware of his qualities before—though I am sure Mr Darcy has always appreciated him at *full* value—we are indeed aware of them now. The smoothness, the ease, of everything at Lyme, has been solely owing to him. So I *will* inform him of the Admiral's dark plot and perhaps," lowering her voice in her turn, "I will tax the Admiral himself with it, if such a thing will not rebound upon his wife?"

Mrs Wentworth solemnly inclined her head.

"It will not rebound upon his wife," she said. "I have to say that, dearly though I love him, I have never seen him in such extravagant spirits here at Lyme and must bestow the credit for that where it is due—that is to say, on the presence of the Darcy family. Having someone to ride with, and go bathing with—for he always said before, you know, that the sea was for sailing *on* rather than for swimming *in*—one did *that* only under compulsion!—has given me back the man I used to know. He is one that cannot be idle and being no longer at sea is a severe trial to him, particularly when actually living beside it. But this year he has even survived his joust with their Lordships and remained in good humour. Do not misunderstand me here. He is never precisely out of humour, but I cannot bear to see him in the glooms as is usual when he returns from London. And it is those glooms which our present company has done so much to dispel."

"Then that can only add to our immense satisfaction in coming to Lyme," said Elizabeth.

They now turned their attention to the little girls, both of whom had expressed a desire to place a bunch of flowers in the hatband of one of the donkeys. All the donkeys wore straw hats, especially constructed to allow their ears to stick through, and this protection enabled them to graze without discomfort in the hottest sun. A band between the ears cried out for decoration and a search for some suitable flowers immediately began.

There were remarkably few. Some knapweed, one stalk of toadflax, a stem of pink yarrow and two heads of something Elizabeth supposed to be a cousin of the dandelion, were all that were to be found. Bound together with a long strand of grass, however, they looked pretty enough and Jane and Anne approached the donkey together. He, however, entirely mistaking their intention, disposed of their bouquet in a single mouthful, at first to their consternation, but then to their great amusement.

"But you have certainly given him a great treat," said Mrs Wentworth. "He could not have found those flowers for himself. Perhaps he will give you a ride later as a reward for your kindness."

"Oh," said Jane, "how lovely that would be. If you please, Mama."

Elizabeth smiled, and said nothing.

The three senior ladies were by now seated at one of the tables. The three gentlemen stood together, talking among themselves but occasionally joining in the talk at the table. Miss Bingley and Miss Crawford sat opposite each another at a second table and Elizabeth and Mrs Wentworth were just in time to overhear the following exchange:

"Your hat is not quite straight, Miss Crawford."

"My hat, Miss Bingley, is not intended to be straight. I am informed by a recent issue of *La Belle Assemblée* that this angle is known as à *l'Italienne*."

"I do not recall seeing hats worn at that angle when I was in Italy last winter."

"And in which part of Italy did you spend last winter?"

"At Leghorn. My sister took a villa."

"Then you may be quite sure that all the women wearing hats at Leghorn were English. They are all a part of Lord Byron's train. I believe that, in the first circles, there is a joking name for them, but grieve to say I know not what it is. And English women abroad are quite famous for the straightness of their hats."

Elizabeth judged it best to intervene at this point and said, perhaps a little too loudly: "We have found a stream in the woods over there, where we may retire if it becomes too hot. I think we could hardly have chosen a better day. This breeze will keep us all comfortable *and* keep the flies away."

She had resigned herself to talking about the weather for some few minutes; but she was spared this necessity by the action of her daughter Jane who, sliding along the bench towards Miss Bingley, said, in an elegant, conversational tone: "Did you know that donkeys' noses were quite soft, Miss Bingley? I did not. Anne and I prepared a nosegay for the hat of one of the donkeys, but he ate it instead and we stroked his nose. It was quite furry, like a blanket. I had expected it to be wet."

"No, I did not," said Miss Bingley, very politely, "but then neither did I know that donkeys wore hats."

"They do in Lyme. They are made of quite prickly straw."

"But what do they do with their ears?" enquired Miss Crawford.

"They have two holes and an ear in each one."

"And are they worn quite straight?" asked Miss Bingley. "Or are they tilted over one eye?"

"Oh, they are quite straight," said Jane, very positively. "They are intended to keep the sun out of both their eyes, you know—not only one of them."

Miss Crawford seemed to be trying not to laugh, but her efforts had no success and she did so without reserve. Elizabeth was always amused by Miss Crawford's laughter and she was especially pleased to hear it at this moment.

"I think that very wise," said Miss Crawford, when she could speak again. "When the dictates of high fashion are *also* followed by donkeys, that will be the time to look about us and wonder where our civilisation is going."

"One of the donkey men plays on a pipe," said Anne.

"And another one has a fiddle," added Jane. "Do you think donkeys like music, Mama?"

"Only if it is especially well played, my love. With such very large ears, I think they would be particularly sensitive to false notes."

Catherine came to sit next to Mrs Wentworth and Mr Elliot shortly requested permission to join them, graciously given by Miss Crawford and by Miss Bingley, who made room for him on her bench.

But, no sooner were they all seated, than Patton came to Elizabeth to ask at what point she would like the champagne to be served.

"The champagne?" she exclaimed, in the greatest astonishment.

"It was brought by Mrs Tilney, madam," said Patton.

XX

Looking up, Elizabeth realised that Mrs Tilney was indeed upon them, wreathed in smiles, wearing a hat which could only have come from the sunbonnet shop, and invested with an air of graciousness which slightly preceded her.

"To whom must I beg forgiveness for my disgraceful behaviour?" she wondered. "The Three Cups is such a source of information—I do not say, you will observe, such a hotbed of gossip—that I could not deny myself this treat once I had heard of it. To be with so many charming friends on this delightful day—I could not let it pass."

Smiling, nodding, she continued: "Miss Bingley—so happy to meet you again. Miss Crawford—I fear I did not recognise you under your bonnet. Mrs Price. Sister Anne. Mrs Darcy. Cousin William! To whom must I present myself, as a friend if not a guest?"

"To the Admiral and Mr Darcy, cousin Elizabeth," said Mr Elliot, not very cordially. "I will take you over."

Then, to Patton: "You had better serve the champagne at once. It will not grow any cooler in the sun."

He took Mrs Tilney by the arm and led her to the other table, leaving everyone at Elizabeth's quite speechless with astonishment. Patton swiftly obeyed his recent instruction and, when they all realised that Mrs Tilney's contribution to their picnic was of the first quality, they were inclined to regard her invasion in a more favourable light. But it left a shadow on their conversation and Elizabeth was particularly grateful for the presence of her own daughters, as it limited them only to the most general topics. She was surprised, and pleased, to see how kind Miss Bingley and Miss Crawford were to Jane and Anne, helping them to all the most delicious dishes and making sure that they missed nothing. Her daughters, she was very amused to find, almost equalled the departed Mrs Tilney in graciousness.

Mr Elliot returned.

"Your sister, cousin Anne, was never renowned for her consideration for other people—neither their feelings nor their convenience. Her taste in champagne, however, is not to be quarrelled with and she can do no harm in the company of Lady Alicia and Mrs Frankland."

He smiled engagingly at them all.

"I hope we may feel able to condone her eccentric conduct."

"I feel ashamed that we did not remember her," said Elizabeth. "I was not sure for how long she intended to stay at Lyme."

"I believe she has not yet decided," said Mr Elliot.

When they had all eaten, their party divided. Lady Alicia, Mrs Frankland and Mrs Grant retired to the Darcys' carriage, where their three parasols were shortly to be seen subsiding on to one another. The Admiral and Mrs Wentworth went into the wood together. Mr Elliot invited Miss Bingley to walk with him and they were shortly joined, after a small exchange of pleasantries, by Mrs Tilney.

"I have just being trying to recall," said Miss Crawford, noticing this, "which of our ancient heroes it was who was torn in pieces by the Harpies. But I am sure your husband will remember."

Mr Darcy now came up, and they went to the other end of the glade with Catherine and Miss Crawford. There Elizabeth, Jane and Anne found a comfortable tree to lean against and, before very long, all three had fallen asleep. Elizabeth woke to find herself smilingly regarded by her husband, her sister, her elder daughter and Miss Crawford. Anne still slumbered quietly on her lap.

"I hope you mean to tell us," said Miss Crawford, "how you contrive to look as handsome when you are asleep as you do when you are awake. And to sleep with your mouth *closed*— *that* I regard as talent of no mean order."

"If you had condescended to fall asleep yourself this afternoon," said Mr Darcy to her, "we might have been able to say the same thing of you."

"Oh no, the risk was too great, with all these people lurking in the woods. Since my friend Flora married, there is no one to tell me how I look when sleeping. It is possible, also, that I *snore*."

Catherine turned to her with a smile.

"Surely Mrs Grant would tell you that?"

"No, indeed. Her room is quite on the other side of the house."

She then placed herself between Elizabeth and Catherine and, taking an arm of each, said in her pleasantest voice: "What a delightful day this has been and how especially happy I have been to spend the afternoon with you. I was afraid, you know, that it would be *my* fate to play gooseberry to Miss Bingley and Mr Elliot. I had a vast deal of experience in that field in days of yore and I should be only too pleased to think that my gooseberrying days were over."

Their appearance in the glade was greeted with a sort of applause. Lady Alicia, hearing of the musicians in their midst, wished to round off the day's festivities with a dance.

"I have crossed their palms with so much silver," said she, "that it has practically turned to gold, but there is a reluctance on the part of the dancers. Can it be that they are too shy to choose their partners?"

"I think that very likely," said Mr Darcy. "I suppose you have a Sir Roger in mind? Let us therefore line up all the men in one row, and all the women in another, and we will take as partner the person opposite."

This suggestion, rather to Elizabeth's surprise, seemed to find favour. Between the footmen, grooms and coachmen it was discovered that they were two women short, Mrs Grant having decided that she was not quite ready for dancing. The innkeeper, too, who had graced the entire proceedings with his presence, said that he preferred to watch. Jane and Anne were turned into ladies in a moment, much to their delight, and Elizabeth shortly found herself standing between them and opposite Miss Bingley's footman. Mr Darcy danced with Alexander on his shoulders and Frances accompanied both Esther and her mother in their turns.

The musicians set a spanking pace. Miss Bingley's hat was soon being worn *a l'Italienne* and Mrs Wentworth avoided any contact with her cousin. The music subtly increased in speed as the dance progressed, the clapping grew louder and louder, the smiles grew broader and broader and there was scarcely a person, at the end of the dance, who was not slightly out of breath.

The last of the champagne, the last of the lemonade, the last of the ale, were all consumed. There were no cakes left and no more fruit. It was time to go home.

The matter of the donkey ride now being raised by both her daughters, Elizabeth approached the donkey man, the one who had been playing the fiddle. He very handsomely offered to convey both children all the way, as his donkey's previous load had been eaten. They were placed side by side on the donkey's back, Jane's legs in the pannier on one side and Anne's in the pannier on the other.

As this drew the attention of both Alexander and Frances, a short consultation with another donkey man, the one who had played the pipe, resulted in their being made quite comfortable inside the baskets themselves. As she waved goodbye to the four beaming children, safely in the care of both James and John, Elizabeth could not altogether help saying to Catherine: "It is a long way through those woods. I believe the smugglers prefer the route towards Charmouth."

"Dearest Lizzy," returned Catherine. "In broad daylight? I believe that smugglers nowadays work only by the light of the full moon."

"It is just that I had not seen them disappear like that, into the trees, you know, before."

They were at home in time to welcome the donkey train, Alexander and Frances now soundly asleep. As they came running up to her, Jane and Anne put in a formal request to have a donkey at Pemberley and Elizabeth could only agree. Mr

Darcy and the Admiral paid off the donkey owners themselves and their picnic came to an end with many smiles and expressions of regret, of satisfaction, and the recollection that there was always another day.

XXI

It was on the day after the day after the picnic that Mrs Wentworth came to call, rather earlier than was quite usual.

"I have to tell you," she said as she sat down, "that my sister has departed and, I have also to say, that a great burden has been lifted—from me."

Realising that her audience was particularly attentive, she went straight on.

"My footman Daniel, as you may not be aware, is in the habit of spending his evenings in the public section of The Three Cups. Here he is, in general, able to meet your admirable Patton and, frequently, your James and John. I understand they make a formidable quartet and that the behaviour in—I believe it to be called the public bar—has improved out of all recognition."

"We are *extremely* pleased to hear it," said Lady Alicia.

"I do not wish to be guilty of gossiping with the servants—and indeed I am not sure if I mean to inform the Admiral since Daniel told me this in confidence—but it is quite certain that my sister left this morning—on what Daniel calls her broomstick."

There was no comment from her hearers. Their attention did not waver.

"I think I may have mentioned," went on Mrs Wentworth, "that my sister, on more than one occasion, dined with Mr Elliot at The Three Cups, under the impression that she was his guest. The reverse, however, turns out to be the truth. They dined together yesterday evening and, either by accident or design as the saying has it, the account was presented to her. A furious argument ensued, bringing, Daniel tells me, complete silence to the public bar. The end of it was that my sister demanded her reckoning *that moment*, and she left, as I told you, this morning. I understand that the public bar is divided in its admiration for the turns of phrase of both parties, Daniel inclining to those of my sister, but," turning to Elizabeth, "Patton thinks my cousin's are superior."

After a very small pause, the laughter began.

"I would much dislike to be the judge in such a case," said Mrs Frankland.

"But," said Mrs Wentworth, "the best is yet to come."

Surveying them all with her most enticing smile, she said: "Mr Elliot is the owner of The Three Cups. It was in the dowry of his wife."

There was a silence, a complete silence.

"So *that* is what brings him to Lyme," said Elizabeth.

"*Not* a large family of children," said Catherine, "though they may be here as well. And the way is now clear for Miss Bingley."

"I cannot quite *place* Miss Bingley," said Lady Alicia. "Does she come only from London—and Leghorn? Or is there some country connection?"

"The family is from Yorkshire," said Elizabeth. "Indeed, I believe there to be a town there of that name. How their father—it is as recent as that—made his money has never been disclosed. But her brother, our dearest sister's loving husband, is *my* husband's oldest friend."

"And do we know what the Admiral thinks of Mr Elliot?" asked Mrs Frankland.

"The Admiral thinks Mr Elliot has an excellent seat upon a horse," said Mrs Wentworth. "I am uncertain of the value of that comment."

It was Ladies' Day. Lady Alicia and Mrs Frankland had hired the bathing machine next to Mrs Tegg's and thither they all repaired, the sun being especially benign. In the evening they dined once more at the inn, a resumption of routine most grateful to them all.

They went, on Sunday, to church as before, and, as before, to Miss Bingley's. Mr Elliot was notable for his absence. Elizabeth had seen the Admiral conversing for some time with

Miss Bingley so that when, on their walk home, he came over and offered her his arm, she made no objection.

"I hope you find Miss Bingley to improve upon acquaintance?" she said. "I have known her for so long that I feel I have nothing further to learn."

"Indeed, Mrs Darcy, is that so?" said the Admiral, with one of his most engaging smiles. "But I think there is a confluence of interest here. My wife informs me that she thinks Miss Bingley at one time wished to marry Mr Darcy—and Mr Elliot, at one time, wished to marry my wife. So how are we, the victors in these old skirmishes, to judge the vanquished with impartiality?"

"I fear you may be right. In all probability we cannot. But if you will give me your opinion of Miss Bingley, I will give you mine of Mr Elliot."

"Bravely said," remarked the Admiral, still smiling. "Will you fire the first salvo, or shall I?"

"I shall," said Elizabeth, very firmly. "All that I know of Mr Elliot I have learned from Mrs Wentworth, an unimpeachable source, and under no circumstances to be challenged. From my own observation he seems to be a man of cool feelings and most unlikely to be led astray by them. He has long had more money than he could comfortably spend and I am therefore inclined to wonder if his present interest in Miss Bingley—for there *is* an interest there; it is quite plain for all to see—does not simply mean that that first fortune may be somewhat in need of repair."

"Shrewdly observed, and sharply," said the Admiral, admiringly. "But from my wife's nearer information, I believe his fortune to be still in excellent case. And from *my* observation of Miss Bingley I think her to be a *woman* of cool feelings and most unlikely to be led astray by them, as you have so skilfully put it. At the same time, I believe there to be a little voice at the back of her head which tells her that it is better to be married than *not* to be married and that now is the time to do something about it."

"I am sure Miss Bingley would have made Mr Darcy most unhappy."

"And I am sure Mr Elliot would have destroyed my wife—not through cruelty or unkindness, I grant you, but rather through a punctiliousness and an unwearying courtesy which, in the end, would have worn her out."

"So we are inclined to think that they deserve each other?"

"We are; and we are also to rejoice that the two people we care for most in the world have not been made miserable by them."

"I seem to recall that Lady Alicia said something similar when she first saw them together."

"Then," said the Admiral with another, triumphant, smile, "we may be quite certain that we are quite right. It will be a privilege to stand by and watch a passage at arms which we can neither promote nor prevent."

Elizabeth was rendered so perfectly comfortable by this conversation that she resolved to put the matter entirely out of her head.

The next day a letter was brought to Catherine from the Receiving Office and she, in turn, brought it to Elizabeth. The last paragraph was as follows:

The house is bright and cheerful. Compared to my Mother's previous residence it is Paradise itself, as she is the first to say. The cook is excellent but the maid-of-all-work, by no means as slovenly as her unregretted predecessor, has little idea how to go on. She is the daughter of one of my father's Marines, notorious for his drunkenness and brutal behaviour to wife and daughters, of whom there are seven, and my Mother, with reason, regards herself as her saviour. She is a pretty and biddable girl who would, if instructed, do perfectly well, but my Mother will not instruct her. I cannot but feel that we should *all* profit from some of your method and can only say that I shall be *most* happy to see you whenever you choose to arrive. Added to which, my very dear, my dearest Catherine, I have only to say how strange it feels to be on shore and not have you beside me. The refit goes well. I trust that all is well at Lyme. My love to them and very much love to you, your ever devoted
William.

There could be no denying such an appeal.

"I had hoped to have you with me the whole month," said Elizabeth, "but here is a situation that cannot be ignored. It must seem curious that Mrs Price cannot order her own household after so many years of practice, but William's meaning is perfectly clear."

"There is irony, too, in the fact that I owe what William calls my method entirely to his sister Susan. It was she who taught me how to go on when first we went to live at Torbay and I think her own knowledge came from inside herself. Perhaps she had only to do exactly what her mother had not done in order to produce the perfect household."

"But you will not wish to go quite immediately, I hope. I know Mrs Grant is anxious that we should all dine with her before you go and that is arranged for Wednesday. Perhaps if you left here on Friday and slept one night on the road, you would arrive on Saturday, when William might be at home. Then the coachman would have Sunday to rest before setting off again."

"The coachman? My dearest Lizzy, I mean to travel post."

"I think you will find Mr Darcy will not hear of that. You are to go in our carriage, with our groom and coachman, but with hired horses all the way. Now, *pray* do not dispute this, dearest Kitty. You will be far more comfortable travelling in this way and we shall have nothing to worry about. It would not surprise me, too, to find that our coachman was truly aching for something to do."

"Well," said Catherine, "I will not dispute it, but I think it a great deal too kind. And Friday will do very well. It will give me time to write to William now and tell him when to expect us— that is to say, if he has given us his direction at Southsea."

He had. The letter was written and posted, and Catherine's departure agreed for Friday.

XXII

Mr Darcy quietly declined Mrs Grant's invitation for Wednesday, considering that the ladies would be happier dining by themselves. He accepted the Admiral's instead, and was to spend the evening with the Wentworths, both at home and at the inn.

The ladies set off to walk to Mr Pyne's house, the evening being particularly fair. They went up the little lane behind the Assembly Rooms, emerging into the bottom of Broad Street; and, as they did so, Elizabeth noticed Mr Elliot coming down the other side of the road, talking very earnestly to a short, stout man, particularly badly dressed.

She was not sure that he *had* seen them and was only half-expecting a bow of acknowledgement; but he continued talking so assiduously to his companion that she began to be certain that he had seen them but was hoping that they had not seen him. She watched them down the hill and round the corner and thought that they turned into Coombe Street.

She said nothing to Mrs Frankland, with whom she was walking; but when Catherine caught up with her, as they went through the archway out of the Shambles, she said to Elizabeth, in a sort of whisper: "Surely that was Mr Elliot just now?"

"Yes," said Elizabeth. "I thought so, too."

"At least *that* companion could not have been his wife."

"No, but perhaps a brother-in-law. And I am quite sure he knew we had seen him."

Their welcome from Mrs Grant and Miss Crawford was as warm as possible.

"It is not quite true to say," said Mrs Grant to Elizabeth, "that I am *pleased* that Mr Darcy chose to dine elsewhere, but I have to admit that I do not know where we should have put him. There is but just room for us six females in Mr Pyne's dining parlour. We shall have to hand the dishes to each other as it is, but we do not have to stand on ceremony with *us*! It is our first real dinner party and I have to say," she went on in a quieter voice, "that it is many, many months since I saw Mary look so well—or so eager for any company."

"She does indeed look quite different from the day we met her first and we take full credit for that," said Elizabeth, not quite seriously.

"As indeed you should," said Mrs Grant. "I do not know when her painting of your family on the beach will be completed but, from the time spent on it, I am sure it will be one of the truly *great* paintings of the decade!"

"We are all getting very impatient," said Elizabeth, laughing. "My sister is to leave on Friday but I would not in any circumstances be thought to hurry the artist."

Their dinner was eaten amid general conversation and to the accompaniment of unrestrained laughter. Elizabeth found herself thinking how much she *was* enjoying herself while she was enjoying herself, rather than remembering her enjoyment afterwards. Miss Crawford was in particularly high spirits and said, rather archly to Elizabeth as she left: "My maid assures me that I do not snore, but can I really rely upon her? We have been together only for seven years. She might not wish to do violence to my feelings."

"I believe," said Elizabeth, taking her cue from Miss Crawford's satirical tone, "that the remedy is to sleep upon one's side, no matter which."

"Truly?" said Miss Crawford. "You are indeed a fountain of information. I suppose all the best solutions are the simple ones."

They returned home, as once before, in a fleet of sedan chairs.

Elizabeth was extremely sad to see Catherine go. While there had been no moments of exceptional intimacy, no discussion of lasting importance, her calm, unhurried presence was one from which everyone could only benefit. She saw her safely installed in the carriage, with Frances delightedly seated between her and Esther. Mr Darcy pronounced the four hired horses unusually handsome and hoped that, if the changes were equally excellent, they should have no difficulty in reaching Ringwood by the evening.

As they walked back down the hill, Mr Darcy took Elizabeth's hand and gave it an especially affectionate squeeze.

"It is quite foolish," said Elizabeth, mopping her eye with her other hand, "to feel sad about Catherine, going, as she is, to a husband who loves her very much. I think my tears must be on my own behalf. I shall miss her."

"You will miss her because you have a loving heart and no one can find fault with that," said Mr Darcy. "But, to cheer you up a little, what will you say when I tell you that my newspaper this morning informs me that Lord Byron set sail for Greece, from Leghorn, on the twenty-fourth of July?"

"I suppose it does not also say," said Elizabeth, brightening at once, "that he took Mrs Hurst and Lady Elliot with him?"

"It certainly does not say that, but, think what one will about his lordship, even he could not be so reckless, so *foolhardy*."

"I expect that they will soon arrive quite destitute at Lyme and fasten on Caroline Bingley."

"They can hardly do so in under a month," said Mr Darcy. "By which time, my dearest Elizabeth, we shall all be safely at home."

This matter was not mentioned at Miss Bingley's on Sunday. Mrs Wentworth remarked on the absence of her cousin for a second time and was told by Miss Bingley that he was thought to have gone to London. There was just enough edge to her voice to prevent the asking of any further questions, and no further questions were asked.

The next day, however, added a new dimension to their lives. No sooner had Mr Darcy returned from his ride than James brought in a letter that he had fetched from the Receiving Office. It had been sent on from Pemberley.

"It is from my cousin Fitzwilliam," said Mr Darcy. "What can he have to say, I wonder? I think we did not even know he had come back to this country."

"'My dear cousin,'" he read aloud, "'I hope you may be pleased to hear that I am returned from Bermuda, quite well but still with a touch of the Bermuda Fever which affects one leg. My brother and his viper-tongued spouse continue as disagreeable as ever and I do not think of going there. They have four daughters already and another in progress—let us hope this may be a son so that they may stop at last. As you may see, I am at my club having nowhere else just now. How soon may I inflict myself upon you and your beautiful wife at Pemberley?'"

Elizabeth did not speak immediately. She had met Colonel Fitzwilliam only once, before her marriage, but she had liked him very much. Her eyes met Mr Darcy's and she said: "Of course he must come here. I do not know what the Bermuda Fever is, precisely, but Lyme seems to have a cure for everything else."

Mr Darcy smiled at her.

"I knew you would say that," he said. "We must think how best it may be contrived."

When the subject was canvassed at nuncheon, Mrs Frankland said at once: "If you would consider conveying us to Bath on Thursday—we may do it not too uncomfortably in a day—in Bath you may hire both coachmen and horses to drive your own carriage to London, once more in one day. That would be Friday. You may return to us, with the Colonel, on Saturday and spend Sunday quietly at home with us. Then on Monday you may arrive here, if you do not choose to sleep at Sherborne. That would depend on the Colonel's state of health, I suppose. Yes," she said, after a little pause, "that would be to combine expedition with comfort, so far as such a thing is possible."

"You will understand from this," said Lady Alicia, with a smile in her voice, "who it was who planned all those successful campaigns in Portugal, though the Great Duke always has the credit. I am quite glad to be sharing my secret with you."

Mr Darcy laughed as he said: "And it would be hard, in this instance, to imagine a more excellent plan. If it is acceptable to you, then it is more than acceptable to me."

An express went off to the Colonel that afternoon.

The carriage came back from Portsmouth on the next day, and with it a letter from Catherine.

The confusion in this house, my dearest Lizzy, is entirely beyond description. Mrs Price sits, nicely dressed on her sofa, engaged in seaming and hem-stitching miles of whitework, I believe for the Seamen's Hospital. Her meals are brought to her there. She seems not to care what she eats or when. Certainly she is always delighted to see Frances and me but I am sure she forgets us as soon as the door is closed. However, Esther and I now propose to put the whole place to rights, and indeed there is nothing else whatever to do, so I hope before long to be comfortable. The one comfort is that Betsy, the youngest daughter, is gone off to her sister at Mansfield, so we are at least spared her constant complaints and evasions.

I should have said before this how *much* I enjoyed myself at Lyme. It was in every way a perfect visit and at least I am come to Portsmouth in the fullest health to deal with all the trouble here. All my most heartfelt thanks. I should mention that the new girl is called Leah, which I think a nice, dependable name and have every hope in time of helping its owner to become a nice, dependable girl. I received a great welcome of a very particular kind from my dearest William. If the great quantity of lobster has had its effect you will certainly have another nephew in the spring. With my love, dearest Lizzy, to you and Mr Darcy and to all the children,

Catherine.

Elizabeth had once or twice started to wonder if the lobster were not having its effect on her, but so far had kept the matter to herself.

They dined with the Wentworths at the inn the night before the party left for Bath, which they did at ten o'clock the next morning. Elizabeth walked up to the carriage with them, aware of a feeling of despondency even though she would certainly see Lady Alicia and Mrs Frankland again on her way through Bath in September.

Their constant high spirits and equable acceptance of every situation made them some of her most valued friends; and she knew she would miss them very much.

She waved them away and her despondency grew, turning to a kind of desolation as she walked down to the house; and this desolation deepened nearly to despair as she saw Miss Bingley, lying in wait for her at the front door.

XXIII

As soon as she was within earshot, Miss Bingley said: "You must forgive this early call. I knew that your guests were leaving today with Mr Darcy, and I most particularly wished to see you alone."

Elizabeth's spirits did not rise very much at this, although she said: "But I am very pleased to see you. One is always a little low after a farewell and Lady Alicia and Mrs Frankland are particular friends. Mr Darcy I expect to see again within the week."

She led the way to the sitting-room and said, with a smile and an amiability that she certainly did not feel: "Now we can be comfortable—and private. Pray sit down and take off your bonnet if you wish."

Miss Bingley sat down but did not take off her bonnet. Elizabeth realised that, for the first time in their acquaintance, Miss Bingley was extremely nervous, as though she were at some disadvantage. After a considerable silence, which Elizabeth did not choose to break, Miss Bingley said: "Mr Elliot has—very properly—asked permission to pay his addresses—to be allowed to be considered a suitor to my hand."

"Then surely I am to congratulate you?"

"But I rather think I have refused him."

"But surely, my dear—Caroline, I have to say, after all these years of formality—there cannot be a 'rather think' in such a case. Either you have. Or you have not."

"Precisely. And it is this which alarms me so. I said he certainly had that permission. He did not specifically ask me to marry him, though I must conclude that that will be his intention in the end. I said only that I would be but too happy to see him whenever he should choose to call and said it as pleasantly as I could."

"Then I do not understand your state of alarm."

"My state of alarm is caused by the fact that I have not seen him from that day to this."

Here was a dilemma for Elizabeth. She did not think she had been mistaken in seeing Mr Elliot in Broad Street on the evening that they dined with Mrs Grant; but to gain a little time, she said: "I understood you to tell us on Sunday that you thought he had gone to London."

"That was merely to account to you for his absence—and to myself, if I am honest. I do not pretend that I am fallen in love with Mr Elliot, but it would be equally foolish to pretend that he has not a great deal to offer."

She turned to Elizabeth with rather a thin smile.

"I have no ambition to be *only* an aunt, you know, charming though your sister's children are."

Taking her courage in both hands, Elizabeth drew a deep breath and said, as kindly as possible: "You are aware, of course, that Mr Elliot has been married before?"

After a half-minute, the studied calm of her face momentarily ruffled, Miss Bingley said: "I was not. Thinking it over, I find I have accepted him entirely at his own value."

"I understood that his wife was a wealthy woman of a lower class, who left him a great deal of both money and property, some of it in Lyme. He has been a widower for nearly ten years."

"Ten years!" said a startled Miss Bingley. "He must have married very young."

"I believe he did, indeed," replied Elizabeth, "and that the marriage could not be described as happy."

A silence fell. Elizabeth, uncertain which way to move, decided to say nothing.

"And in those ten years?" said Miss Bingley, at last. "I must suppose—a mistress?"

"The Mrs Clay who caused his exit from our Assembly Ball. In the end, he sent her back to her father with only the money for her journey."

Miss Bingley merely looked her amazement.

"A not inconsiderable sum," remarked Elizabeth, lightly. "They lived together in London and her father is in Somerset."

"Mr Elliot has a house in Park Street."

Elizabeth was still in a quandary. On the one hand, her conscience told her that she should tell Miss Bingley that she had seen Mr Elliot in Lyme a week ago. On the other, she did not wish to do anything to discourage what seemed to her to be a very desirable match.

"We do not know, I imagine, what kind of property Mr Elliot's wife left him," said Miss Bingley. "It could only be houses, I think, as there seems to be no industry in Lyme, except perhaps for the cloth manufactory on Mill Green."

"We have known Mr Elliot no longer than you. We met Sir Walter and Lady Elliot in Bath three years ago, but all my information comes from Mrs Wentworth, his cousin, so I have no reason to question it."

"He seemed quite well-known to the Master of Ceremonies in the Assembly Rooms."

"A frequent visitor, then?"

"Perhaps."

"It *is* very perplexing," said Elizabeth, with as much warmth in her voice as she could manage, "and, I am inclined to think, quite out of character with him. But perhaps we should remember that we do not know definitely that he is not in London. Could he have gone to consult his attorney?"

Miss Bingley brightened quite visibly.

"That I had *not* considered—though I might regard it as a thought premature."

"It would be idle of me," said Elizabeth, "to pretend that this matter has not received some discussion amongst us, and this seems the moment to tell you that Lady Alicia and Mrs Frankland, who have known Mr Elliot a great while, think you should not proceed without the assistance of *your* attorney."

Miss Bingley was suddenly all attention.

"You cannot mean—they cannot mean—that Mr Elliot is all to pieces?"

Elizabeth contemplated this for a moment.

"Well, I will certainly not disguise from *you*," she said at last, "that the thought had presented itself to *me*."

"How strange life is," remarked Miss Bingley. "Ten years ago the idea of being married for my money was quite a commonplace. And my sister certainly was. Now the prospect of such a thing seems perfectly repugnant."

"I wonder if your newspaper carried the information that Lord Byron had left Leghorn for Greece some two weeks ago?"

"No," said Miss Bingley, in a lower, downcast voice. "It did not."

As the pause in the conversation seemed unlikely to end for some time, Elizabeth rang the bell. When it was answered, she asked for some lemonade to be brought in. Its arrival created an acceptable disturbance, and they both drank it gratefully.

It was at this moment that Mrs Wentworth was ushered into the room. Elizabeth, surprised and delighted, had just presence of mind enough to ask for some more lemonade, and this was brought in immediately.

Mrs Wentworth settled on a chair by the window, opposite Miss Bingley but at some distance from Elizabeth. She took one sip of lemonade and then put down her glass.

"It is a particularly beautiful day," she said. "One must hope that our travellers will benefit from it. But I find myself sitting here not questioning, for once, but believing in, the dispensations of Providence."

She smiled at Miss Bingley.

"I have this morning sustained—I should say *we* have sustained—a visit from my cousin William Elliot. I came here to discuss what had transpired with Elizabeth, as *your* friend, Miss Bingley. But, as you are here yourself, I think it kinder to discuss his situation quite directly with you."

"I should be most grateful, indeed," said Miss Bingley, but in a rather distant tone. "I am here myself on the same errand."

Mrs Wentworth took a longer drink of lemonade and then said: "It is a tale. You must make yourselves comfortable."

Then, as neither of the others moved, she began.

"Twice in his life Mr William Elliot has quarrelled with my father, who must be considered as the head of his family.

The first time was on the occasion of his own marriage when, instead of marrying my sister Elizabeth, as my father undoubtedly intended, he married for money, but money that had been obtained—I do not say illegally, but in rather unfashionable, if not unsavoury, ways. There was a complete rupture. Then, when his wife died, he was re-admitted to the family but on the tacit understanding that he would *now* marry Elizabeth, who was still single. Most unfortunately, however, he preferred me to her and my heart, as we know, was given elsewhere. Mr Elliot retired, taking with him a friend of Elizabeth's, a Mrs Clay, whom I had thought to have marriage with my father in her view. So there was another absolute breach."

She turned to Elizabeth. "I fear that much of this is known to you, but as we are all in this situation together, I must ask you to be patient. This second rupture was further deepened on the occasion of my *father's* marriage, when Mr Elliot sent him the rudest letter it has ever been my privilege to read. He could, I am inclined to think, do well as editor of some polemical journal. And my poor stepmother, shrewd and fairly vulgar as she undoubtedly is, did not in fact deserve any of the words he used about her. She gave my father three sons and cleared his debts. She had been brought up to count her pennies and now she counted his. I cannot at all regret her brief reign as my father's wife. But the rift, the rupture, the breach, with Mr Elliot, one now supposed to be permanent."

She took another sip of lemonade and then turned to smile at Miss Bingley.

"Mr Elliot, it now transpires, wishes to become a leader in fashionable society, though he would not use those words himself. For this, he requires an impeccable wife, and he is under the impression that he has now discovered someone to occupy that desirable situation. He is in Lyme to sell off all the remnants of his first wife's fortune—which include, you may be astonished to hear, an interest in the Cloth Mill, an interest in the Assembly Rooms and an interest in The Three Cups. When he has done this, he will once again apply to the lady who is to become his impeccable wife, hope she will accept him and hope also that we—that is to say, the Admiral and I—will act to replace him in the good graces of my father. Quite why this should be such a matter of importance to him I am uncertain, but then I also do not know what credentials are demanded of a leader of fashion."

Miss Bingley had sat as though paralysed throughout this recital. Now she moved, just sufficiently to give herself a sip of lemonade.

"Well," she said, at last, "I must not pretend to misunderstand you. Mr Elliot is good-looking, perfectly healthy so far as one may judge, and as rich as he needs to be. Women very often believe that they will change the men they marry but this is very rarely the case. My sister certainly did so, but not one ingrained habit did she alter. The impression of Mr Elliot that I have now received from Mrs Wentworth is that he is a selfish, vain, ambitious man. Would you agree with this?"

"You put it very plainly, Miss Bingley," said Mrs Wentworth.

"So what advice would you offer to one who is contemplating marriage with such a man?"

"The only sovereign remedy would be to become even more selfish, vain and ambitious than he," said Elizabeth, rather sharply. "But this," she added more kindly, "I think you would be most unwise to attempt. If you are aware of these—faults, I think I have to call them—you are the more easily able to counteract them."

"She speaks very truly," said Mrs Wentworth to Miss Bingley. "Mr Elliot's faults are, I am persuaded, mostly superficial. I believe there to be an excellent man underneath. His courtship of myself, however unwelcome at the time, I can never wholly forget."

"But," said Elizabeth, "you must consult your attorney."

"I can hardly go alone to London to do that."

"You can summon him to Lyme. If you need a chaperon at Monmouth House I will certainly oblige. But of course he can go to an inn."

This aspect of the matter did not seem to have occurred to Miss Bingley.

"My money is so entangled with trusts and trustees that it would take a cleverer man than Mr Elliot to run off with it, I think," said Miss Bingley.

"You must forgive me for saying *this*," said Mrs Wentworth, urgently, "but you would be *most* unwise to believe that."

There seemed little to say after this. Miss Bingley rose and Miss Bingley smiled. Elizabeth was once more surprised to see how handsome she could be when looking pleasant.

"I am—obliged—to you both," she said, with an effort. "I think I now know how best to proceed."

She left a silence behind her in the room. The two remaining gazed at each other without speaking and rather absently sipped their lemonade. Then Mrs Wentworth said: "I would have called today in any case—to ask how *you* are feeling in the morning?"

"Never better, I am thankful to say. But—oh, it is the lobster after all? Am I to congratulate you?"

"It is very early yet, of course. But if it is what I think it is, I never felt like this with the other two."

"You must take the greatest care of yourself. Do you think it is now time to stop our diet of lobster?"

"I do not indeed. I suppose it is unobtainable when you are at home, just as it is with us? Make hay, they say, while the sun shines. Eat lobster, I think, when at the seaside."

"And no one could disagree with that."

After a moment, Elizabeth said: "I appeal to you for guidance, Mrs Wentworth. Should I be feeling sorry for Mr Elliot, or for Miss Bingley? Or should I be rejoicing at the prospect of this perfect connubial union—which is to be such an example to us all?"

"You must drop the Mrs Wentworth, please. And I feel myself so inclined to laugh immoderately at the entire situation, that I cannot help but wonder if there is not some secret ingredient in your lemonade."

They laughed together, not quite immoderately; and finished the lemonade.

XXIV

E lizabeth went to Church only with the Wentworths and was particularly conscious of the emptiness of their pew. Once more Mr Elliot was not there. Once more Miss Bingley invited them in.

The Admiral went ahead with Miss Bingley, leaving Elizabeth and Mrs Wentworth to walk together. They had hardly crossed the Church Road into Monmouth Street when they saw Mr Elliot approaching from its other end.

"Setting out to meet us accidentally," said Elizabeth, very quietly to Mrs Wentworth. "But he would have done better to meet us in Church, as befits the pattern of perfection that he proposes to be."

Mr Elliot was invited in. He came over to speak to Elizabeth and Mrs Wentworth, who were standing together by the window.

"I hope you mean to congratulate me, cousin Anne," he said. "I have this morning agreed the sale of my interest in the Cloth Mill."

"Then I do congratulate you," said Mrs Wentworth. "I hope this does not mean that the fortunes of the Mill will descend even further? Agreements made upon a Sunday, you know, are not supposed to prosper."

"By no means," said Mr Elliot, his smile just a little too charming, Elizabeth thought, for the occasion. "He is an energetic man who knows his business. I believe he will revive, if not precisely restore, its fortunes. I have sometimes felt that I should involve myself more personally, but was always disinclined to do so. I must hope that all my interests in Lyme will pass to better hands."

"I like your modesty," said Mrs Wentworth, but not with much conviction, "and do most sincerely share your hope."

Mr Elliot turned to Elizabeth: "I had the great pleasure of attending your ball for Miss de Bourgh earlier this year, Mrs Darcy. I hope you will allow me to say that it was quite one of the more enjoyable festivities of the recent season. May we perhaps hope that you mean to do something of the sort each year?"

Elizabeth, completely taken aback, tried not to look as startled as she felt.

"I think I must make no rash promises of the kind," she said, "especially not to one who might, in future, hold me to them. My husband's cousin, Miss de Bourgh, is our very particular friend and my elder daughter, as you may not know, is not yet eight years old."

"Whoever undertook to refurbish that house in Brook Street must certainly be congratulated on their success."

"To that I may plead guilty myself, Mr Elliot, and I am, of course, charmed to hear you say so."

"I understand, from one of my older acquaintance, that it was the first time the house had been opened since the death of Lady Anne Darcy. She described it to me as a mausoleum."

"It was indeed very dark and, if I may so put it, a little moth-eaten. But there was a satisfaction in bringing it back to life."

"And now that you have done so, so skilfully, may one petition that it should be opened at regular intervals? With so many newcomers on the social scene, newcomers from all corners of society, one should add, it must be the prerogative of the older country families to show the mushrooms how to behave."

"That would hardly be an adequate reason for giving a ball, my dear cousin," said Mrs Wentworth. "Indeed I cannot think of a better one for *not* doing so. But you might think of writing a manual on the subject yourself."

Mr Elliot looked as though he thought this an excellent notion. Elizabeth was somewhat at Mr Elliot's mercy, since she had no means of knowing whether he had attended her ball or not, although he had scraped acquaintance at the Assembly Ball.

"Well, I will promise you, Mr Elliot," she said, with a smile directed only to him, "as a special favour, to give at least one more ball before the come-out of my daughter Jane—which will be, if my arithmetic is correct, in 1834."

They were all able to laugh at this and the Admiral came over to discover what they laughed about. Elizabeth swiftly detached herself and went over to Miss Bingley, who greeted her with an almost welcoming smile.

"I have sent for my attorney," was all she said. "He should be here on Tuesday."

"I hope you may find that there is a perfectly rational explanation, firstly for the sudden disappearance and, secondly, for this re-appearance."

"I hope so, too," said Miss Bingley. Then, picking up a plate of very small cakes, thickly topped with soft white icing, she said, with something approaching a gleam in her eye: "Let us eat these *all* by ourselves."

They did so. But Elizabeth was not allowed to escape further conversation with Mr Elliot. He came up to her and said, as they were preparing to leave: "I am sorry that Mr Darcy should not be here today, and sorry, too, that his errand to London should be such a sad one."

"I have no knowledge of the Bermuda Fever," returned Elizabeth. "But I trust he is not so very ill."

"I have not yet met Colonel Fitzwilliam," said Mr Elliot. "His brother, the Earl, is well-known in society principally for his wife—one of the plainest, richest and most caustic-tongued women in the kingdom."

"With the present state of things in London," remarked the Admiral, overhearing this, "one might almost say that that approximated to a compliment."

Elizabeth dined at the inn that evening and, on the following afternoon, the tide being right, went with Rebecca and the children to the Pool. She was particularly conscious of Mr Darcy's absence on this occasion, especially as she was very unhandy at making castles in the sand; but the heroine of the day proved to be Rebecca who, armed with Mr Darcy's spade, raised a castle of such spectacular size and grandeur that it was applauded by passers-by above them on the Cobb. Not until it was swept away by the encroaching sea, to the loudly-expressed dissatisfaction of almost everyone who observed it, did they gather themselves up and return home.

As they were very nearly at their own front door, it was Jane who said: "Look, Mama. Papa."

And off she went to meet him.

Elizabeth, wind-swept and sand-blown as she was, waited for them to arrive, delighted that they should have done so a full two hours before they were expected. Colonel Fitzwilliam was pale and limped a little, both somewhat emphasised by his proximity to Mr Darcy, a picture of health, and whose good looks could still, on occasion, take Elizabeth by surprise.

When the arrival was over, Colonel Fitzwilliam's gear bestowed next door, and Elizabeth's own hair hastily tidied, they settled in the sitting-room. After a small discussion, some tea was brought in for Elizabeth and some beer for the gentlemen; but they had hardly time to sample these before the door opened, and Miss Crawford came into the room.

She carried a flat, rectangular parcel under one arm but, as soon as she saw Colonel Fitzwilliam, she stopped, and almost dropped it.

"Henry Fitzwilliam," she said, before anyone could speak.

Colonel Fitzwilliam rose with some difficulty.

"Mary Crawford," he said; and a complete silence fell.

"Usually," said Miss Crawford, swiftly recovering herself, "one says 'I hope I see you well'. But you, my dear friend, if my eyes do not deceive me, are by no means well at all. I hope it is nothing very serious?"

"A touch of fever," said Colonel Fitzwilliam. "And I am sure it will soon pass. I am just returned from the Bermudas."

"From the Bermudas!" exclaimed Miss Crawford. "So that was where you went."

They both sat down, the one opposite the other. Elizabeth had the extraordinary feeling that she and Mr Darcy had become invisible, that the two others were now unaware of their presence.

"Then—tell me," said Colonel Fitzwilliam. "Flora—Miss Ross—Lady Stornaway. How is she?"

"Flora—Miss Ross—Lady Stornaway," said Miss Crawford, in a very level voice, "died in a hunting accident. It will be three years ago in November. There was a small scandal attached to her death, but not one of sufficient size, perhaps, to warrant inclusion among the pages of the *Bermuda Gazette*, should there happen to be such a thing."

"There does happen to be such a thing," said Colonel Fitzwilliam, "but it did not carry that information. She was no horse-woman formerly."

"No, she was not," conceded Miss Crawford. "But, no sooner had she given him two sons, than Lord Stornaway insisted on her presence in the hunting field. He had her money and he had two heirs. He was a—bruising rider himself and had little patience with those who were not."

"I should like to hear the whole," said Colonel Fitzwilliam.

"I never liked Lord Stornaway," said Miss Crawford coolly. "He had nothing to recommend him but his blackguard looks and, undoubtedly, in hunting rig upon a horse, he was a sight to draw all eyes. But that could not compensate for a marriage that was, in every other respect and on Flora's side, a simple tale of misery, neglect—and cruelty."

"Continue."

"She, poor deluded simpleton that she was, found that the one way to please him was to hunt alongside him, taking fence for fence and ditch for ditch. She would arrive already—fortified—and would partake liberally of the stirrup cup, starting off with her judgment seriously at odds. Surprisingly enough, she had no mishap until the final one. She and Lord Stornaway jumped a hedge together, but there was a wide ditch on the far side of it and she fell. And broke her neck. It was instant. Lord Stornaway himself was uninjured, but the whole episode was held to be his fault—he had obliged her to overface her horse."

Colonel Fitzwilliam did not speak.

"And there the matter might have rested," continued Miss Crawford after a moment, and almost reminiscently, "but, being away from home, she was not laid out by her own people. And her body was found to be frequently covered by marks that could only have been made with a whip."

Colonel Fitzwilliam stirred in his seat.

"My dear Mary," he said, "I hope you do not mean—?"

"There could be no proof, of course, but there could be only one supposition. And Lord Stornaway very soon found it convenient to retire to his Scottish estates where, so far as I am aware, he remains. But my heart bleeds for those two little boys."

"Scot-free!" exclaimed Colonel Fitzwilliam. "Would I had been there. Did no one offer to punish him?"

"Not in that way," said Miss Crawford. "But the cut direct, formally administered, is a painful thing. The invitations that do not arrive. An escort to the door of a club. Polite society has its weapons and it used them all upon Lord Stornaway. It would surprise me if he ever appeared in London again."

A silence fell, but Elizabeth did not choose to disturb it. Mr Darcy also sat quietly, absorbing every word.

"And you, Henry Fitzwilliam?" said Miss Crawford, after some time. "What happened to you? May I say in my own defence—as the almost professional gooseberry that I had become—that I begged Flora on my knees to accept your proposal. But there seemed to be nothing I could say."

"I sold out," said Colonel Fitzwilliam, almost brusquely, "of one Regiment, the Blues, if you remember, and into another— the 57th Foot, knowing they were soon to be drafted overseas. I was out of England within the fortnight. We were for some time in Canada, for the last five years in Bermuda."

Elizabeth was deeply saddened to see the tears falling softly down Miss Crawford's cheeks, but judged it wiser not to intervene.

"I looked for you," Miss Crawford said. "I hoped you might come to see me. You vanished."

"I did. I intended to. It seems I overlooked our gooseberry which, at this moment, I much regret. But at the time I wanted

LAURENCE FLEMING

only to start again, with nothing, no one, that could remind me of what had passed. Even now, with seeing you again, I find the wound is still quite fresh."

Elizabeth and Mr Darcy now rose as one person. Mr Darcy re-filled Colonel Fitzwilliam's tankard and Elizabeth quietly removed the parcel from Miss Crawford's grasp. She was still clutching it. Then she led her over to the table and poured her out a cup of tea. A profound silence filled the room.

It was fully five minutes before the apologies began.

"I am sorry—" said Colonel Fitzwilliam.

"You must forgive—" said Miss Crawford, at the same time.

But Mr Darcy said, above them both, that they had no need to say another word.

"The situation is quite plain," he said. "On our side we can only say that, had we known of your prior acquaintance, we could never have sprung this meeting upon you in this way."

"The Wentworths dine with us this evening," said Elizabeth to Miss Crawford. "I hope that you will stay to meet them? If you would like to come upstairs with me now," she added in a lower voice, "we could remove all traces of those tears."

XXV

B ut upstairs the tears continued. Alone with Elizabeth, there was no longer a need for restraint. Miss Crawford, sitting on a chair by the window, gave way to her grief.

Elizabeth left the room as unobtrusively as possible. She found Jemima and sent her to Mrs Maltby, to make an egg-in-brandy. At the same time she sent a note to Mrs Grant.

Miss Crawford's sobs were plainly to be heard in the nursery. Elizabeth could only hope that they could not be so down-stairs, deep-seated and heart-rending as they were. Asking her children to play as quietly as possible, she returned to her room to find Miss Crawford rather calmer. The egg-in-brandy arriving at precisely that moment, Elizabeth gently compelled her to drink it; and, in a minute or two, Miss Crawford produced an uncertain smile.

"I am ashamed of my noise," she said, "but not displeased that I can make it."

She handed back the glass to Elizabeth and said, more firmly: "Thank you. I do not think there is another person in the world whom I could have endured as witness to my tears. I am entirely taken by surprise. Pray, how does Henry Fitzwilliam come to be sitting in your house?"

"He is first cousin to Mr Darcy—whose own name, as you may not know, is Fitzwilliam."

"It must be quite nine years ago," remarked Miss Crawford, "while I still lived with my uncle, the Admiral, before I ever went to Mansfield. The wound must have been very deep if it is still bleeding after so long."

Elizabeth said only: "Yes."

"I was, I think, a very thoughtless, heedless, inconsiderate girl," said Miss Crawford presently, "as certainly was my great friend Flora. But I could have salved the wound for Colonel

Fitzwilliam, as I must suppose him still to be, if only he had come to me. I could have told him he was given up simply for a greater title, dreadful though it now seems to admit it. That was Flora's sole reservation about him. She was surely punished for her decision—*more* than enough, we can undoubtedly say."

There was only one chair in that small room. Elizabeth sat down on the bed. Miss Crawford continued to speak absently, almost as though she were talking to herself.

"He was very handsome, very dashing. If his passion for Flora had not been so perfectly plain, I would have welcomed his glance in my direction. Indeed, if truth be told, I had hoped that that might happen when Flora gave him her answer. But I think it the common fate of gooseberries to be invisible—and indeed, from his own account just now, not only was he out of London very soon, he was also out of England. I am quite horrified to see him as he is. How long has he been so ill?"

"That we do not know," said Elizabeth. "He is but just arrived. We hope that Lyme may cure him."

"I should have made sad work of being a clergyman's wife," said Miss Crawford quietly. "I wonder now that I should ever have considered it, except that I can see the resemblance between the Henry Fitzwilliam that I knew and Mr Edmund Bertram. Perhaps there was always a preference there that I did not choose to acknowledge. I am sure there is no Bourbon blood in me. I forget nothing but I think I learn something— that is to say, I hope I do."

She turned to face Elizabeth and said, in a voice not quite her own: "I was reared to regard marriage as a duty, not necessarily a very pleasant one. The people I knew had married for convenience, or because the family insisted, or because their estates marched. Never did I encounter what might pass as a contented couple. My aunt and uncle lived entirely separate lives. They met only at dinner when he would make remarks to her that should have been addressed to the cook, would advise her to turn off a footman whose face he did not like, or would comment unpleasantly on the way she had spent her day, however that had been. I think it never entered our heads that there could be any happiness in marriage. Our function was to find a husband before we turned twenty, and if we were steered in the direction of Lord Such-and-such, who was old, ugly and with a dead wife and two daughters but an unencumbered estate, we were willing to be so steered. No matter that the Honourable George So-and-so, young, handsome, *agreeable* and impoverished was standing smiling by the wayside—he was invisible to us all. I do not think our feelings were ever mentioned and certainly, speaking for myself, I do not think I knew I had any."

She sat up more erectly in her chair and said: "Well, that is to let my hair down with a vengeance indeed. I fear that it may all be but too true. Now, with my observation of you and Mr Darcy, and indeed of the Wentworths, I begin to see that there may be something in it—that marriage can be both pleasant and companionable."

Elizabeth nodded.

"I hold myself extremely fortunate," she said, "to have the husband that I have, to love him as I do and to be loved in return. Mrs Wentworth, I venture to suggest, would probably agree. But you must not think we do not understand our good luck."

They sat in silence for some time. There was nothing that had to be said, no comfort that had to be offered, or indeed that could be offered, and gradually Miss Crawford regained her calm, her poise, her customary *sangfroid*.

"The Fitzwilliams, or the Belfords I should rather say, have not two farthings of their own, as no doubt you know," she said at last, quite in her own decisive voice. "They own half a county in the north which will just, in a very good season, support two cows, four sheep and a flock of geese—they are obliged *always* to marry money. But I think I am rich enough for a younger son. I should not want to live at Everingham—not, I think, ever again and in any case it is leased for fifteen years. So where would we live, I wonder? Do you think I could endure a villa at Sidmouth? Or Dawlish? Or Cromer?"

Elizabeth was now brave enough to laugh, more than happy to find Miss Crawford returned to her usual self.

"No," she said, "I do not. I think you would be more comfortable in a villa by the Thames."

"But *not* at Twickenham," said Miss Crawford immediately. "Too many memories there."

"If you would exchange your river for a canal, I believe they are building many desirable residences in the Regent's Park."

"Now there you speak like a sensible woman. But we are a little ahead of ourselves, are we not? The result of my spoken meditation must principally be to learn that, in the vulgar phrase, if the Colonel should choose to throw his handkerchief at me, I should be much inclined to pick it up."

"And you will believe me when I say that I must hope, indeed, that he will do so very soon."

More practical counsels now prevailed. Rebecca and Jemima were summoned. Both Elizabeth and Miss Crawford had their hair done, to conflicting instructions from Jane and Anne, seated on the bed. Elizabeth, still in the calico wrapper she had worn on the beach, put on something more formal. A shawl was found for Miss Crawford to wear over her afternoon dress and, all traces of emotion completely removed, they prepared to go downstairs.

"We will just wait," said Elizabeth, "until we see the Wentworths coming up the hill. In many ways this is a most convenient window. For this first evening, I rather think, there must be safety in numbers."

Almost as she spoke, the Wentworths came into view, Elizabeth thinking, once again, what an elegant couple they made.

"We will count to thirty," she said quietly to Miss Crawford, "and then go down and meet them at the door."

XXVI

Their plan succeeded. In the sitting-room, Mr Darcy presented Colonel Fitzwilliam and then they all sat down; but no sooner was she seated than Mrs Wentworth exclaimed: "The parcel! Surely I espy a parcel of precisely the size and shape to contain Miss Crawford's portrait of the Darcy family?"

Then, to Elizabeth: "How can you endure to sit there with it still unwrapped?"

And to Miss Crawford: "Pray, pray, put us out of our agony and perform the unveiling ceremony."

Miss Crawford got up, smiling, and said in a low voice to Elizabeth: "Indeed, I had forgot all about it."

Then, rather more loudly: "I had intended to do so in private but can only hope that my little painting be worthy of this wider audience."

And so it proved. Elizabeth, noticing that Miss Crawford was still trembling, helped her with the unwrapping and the painting was revealed, fresh and sparkling, in an elegant, flattering frame.

For a moment, there was silence. Then the chorus of praise began, the loudest voice unquestionably that of Colonel Fitzwilliam.

"My dear Mary," he said, "I am most truly amazed. No one who knew you before could have guessed at such skill, such taste. I have only glimpsed your children, Fitzwilliam, but surely she has caught them perfectly? And that way you have of wearing your hat makes you look devilish handsome—I must try it myself. But where is Mrs Darcy? Where is Elizabeth?"

"My sister and I are these two figures in the foreground," said Elizabeth. "It is a speaking likeness of both our bonnets.

And as for the sea and the hills beyond Lyme, I could look at them for ever."

When the excitement had subsided a little, Miss Crawford took the painting and presented it to Elizabeth, with a smile and a curtsey. Elizabeth, smiling and curtseying in return, said it would be one of their greatest treasures.

"And I know just where I shall put it—where I can see it from my bed, with its back to the light, above my dressing-table."

The evening passed effortlessly. Champagne was served with dinner. The conversation never faltered and Mrs Maltby seemed even to have excelled herself. Elizabeth's spirits rose and rose as one superb dish followed another and she was particularly pleased to see Colonel Fitzwilliam doing justice to them all. As they waited for the second course, the Admiral said: "But what is this I hear about Bermuda Fever, Colonel? I was on the Bermuda Station for some years, though some time ago undoubtedly. I do not recall any talk of fever then. Indeed, the place was thought to be particularly healthy. All the wives and children with us there bloomed like—roses, I was going to say, but, however, like the lilies that grow so well there."

"You may perhaps remember, Admiral, that there is no water on the islands?" replied the Colonel. "All the water must be trapped and stored, only rainwater, you know, and it is thought that some infection entered one of the tanks. All those afflicted with the fever had drunk the same water—all were from the same tribe, the same parish—all from Pembroke."

"Well, at least you are come to the best place to recover from a Bermuda Fever," said the Admiral. "Sir George Somer, who first named the islands, was native to Lyme. I feel sure he is putting in a good word for you."

"Was he so?" asked the Colonel. "Then it only increases the enormous satisfaction I already feel in being here."

"I fear," said the Admiral, half-laughing to Mr Darcy, "that the Colonel's arrival means that I must surrender my seat on your horse?"

"No, indeed, it does not. My poor cousin is ordered to *walk*, to release the stiffness in his knee. He is ordered into the sea as well, but that cannot happen until Wednesday."

"I foresee an exhausting time ahead of me—but think I feel better already," said the Colonel, not quite seriously. "There seems to be a very good air."

"Compared to the air in London," said Miss Crawford, "the air here is quite excellent. Indeed all air is excellent compared to the air in London. One feels that, there, it has all been breathed before, and by no means only by human beings. I hope you were not there for very long?"

Through the laughter, and murmurs of protest, Colonel Fitzwilliam was heard to say: "A little over the four weeks."

"Then it is no wonder, my dear Henry, if I may continue so to call you, that you are looking so extremely pale," said Miss Crawford. "We must not heap all the blame upon Bermuda."

When the ladies retired, and were settled alone in the sitting-room, Mrs Wentworth said, with a particularly radiant smile: "I am no longer in any doubt, my dear Elizabeth. I go through purgatory every morning but I hope the lobster may have done its work. You may say a little prayer for me."

"And that I most certainly will," said Elizabeth, "if you will say the same prayer for me."

They laughed together.

"If we *do* succeed," said Mrs Wentworth, "we must send some kind of recognition to Catherine's herb-woman. Though I cannot imagine of what kind."

"Catherine herself, I rather fancy, is somewhat in the same case. Truly the lobster has much to answer for."

They now took Miss Crawford into their confidence and talked of nothing else until the gentlemen could be heard rising.

"I have not told the Admiral," said Mrs Wentworth. "It is too early to be all wrapped up in cotton."

"And I have not told Mr Darcy—for the same reason."

"Then I undertake not to say a word," said Miss Crawford.

"I have never asked how long you remain in Lyme?" said Mrs Wentworth suddenly.

"Until the last day of this month," said Elizabeth. "Then there are pheasants at Pemberley, and so many that one can almost hear them from here. And all the gentlemen in Derbyshire are coming to shoot them."

"And Miss Crawford?"

"I believe that remains to be seen," said Miss Crawford rather uncertainly. "But my sister proposes to spend the winter here."

Miss Crawford did not stay long after the tea and coffee were brought in. A chair was sent for and she was escorted on her journey by both James and John. Not long afterwards Mrs Wentworth observed, as kindly as possible, that she thought the Colonel, after such a long journey, might be better off in bed; and she and the Admiral accompanied him to his front door, on their way back down the hill.

XXVII

No sooner had the breakfast dishes been removed the next day than Patton came into the room.

"I have to inform you, sir, madam, that Colonel Fitzwilliam passed a particularly disturbed night. His man told me of it and I have taken the liberty of sending for a doctor recommended to me by Mrs Sidford. He should already be on his way."

"Thank you, Patton," said Mr Darcy. "I am sure that we are both grateful to you for allowing us to breakfast in peace. But we must go to his house immediately."

There was little to be done in the lower house. The Colonel lay in bed breathing heavily and with an occasional sweat appearing on his brow. Elizabeth took over the duty of wiping this away while Mr Darcy questioned the Colonel's man, an old soldier who had been with him both in Canada and Bermuda.

"He began shouting in early morning," he said. "Not making any sense. But I do not think, with all respect, that it is the Bermuda Fever. That brought with it red blotches on the face."

"Then we must be grateful for that," said Mr Darcy. "You think it may be something from London?"

"Colonel was very weak when we arrived. Four weeks in London don't improve the health."

"Most certainly not. In general one can only admit that it does not."

The doctor came, a little too optimistic for Elizabeth's taste. He advised keeping the patient warm, but not too hot, and prescribed regular saline draughts, which he would have sent over from the apothecary. They could only acquiesce.

Elizabeth decided to remain while they waited for the draughts to arrive. She sat on one side of the bed, with the Colonel's man on the other.

"Foston, madam," he said, in answer to her unspoken question. "Thomas Foston. As devoted to the Colonel as anyone could be."

"Were you with him when first he went to Canada?"

"I was, madam, and always understood why he went. Would like to meet that girl—Flora her name was—and give her a piece of my mind. Used to shout her name in his sleep. But not last night. Sounded more like Runaway or Gornaway—something like that."

"Stornaway," said Elizabeth. "Flora married Lord Stornaway, who was very unkind to her. She is no longer with us and has been punished quite enough."

"I try to be sorry to hear it," said Foston, unsmiling.

As they sat in silence, unable to do anything, the Colonel continued his heavy breathing; but he remained, to Elizabeth's eyes, alarmingly still. So when, a little later, there was a knock at the door, she decided to answer it herself.

It was Mrs Tegg, rather red in the face, and carrying a wooden bucket covered with a cloth.

"I hears," she said at once. "One of them nasty foreign fevers—or just from London. Tegg got you some of this, Mermaid's Tresses we calls it, seaweed from below the tide. You sends it to Mrs Wicken, goat lady. She makes a syrup from it, supped regular, and also in a cheese. She knows. And goat curd and goat whey. You send her some pans."

Elizabeth was aware not only that a great favour was being bestowed, but also that it was a direct command which was not to be ignored.

"I am more obliged to you than I can say," she said, taking the bucket from her. "I will do exactly what you tell me."

"You will be very wise," said Mrs Tegg.

John and James were swiftly summoned. Mrs Sibford supplied the pans and they were sent off together, to bring back anything that could be supplied that day. Elizabeth was about to go back upstairs, when Mrs Wentworth knocked and entered.

"In my house, you know," she said, smiling, "I must always be aware of any ripples on the surface of our life in Lyme. I had hoped the source of today's ripples might not be here—but now I must fear that it is."

"The Colonel is in a deep, unhealthy sleep," said Elizabeth, "and we are afraid to wake him."

"I thought it might be something of the kind," said Mrs Wentworth. "I have brought my lavender vinaigrette if you think it could be of use."

They went upstairs together, to persuade Foston to leave them and try to get some sleep.

"I think," said Mrs Wentworth to him, "that it may be night duty for you for some time. If you will trust us to do the days."

"I will, madam," he said. "And I thank you."

Elizabeth now remembered that it was her bathing day. Leaving Mrs Wentworth in charge, she went back to find both Rebecca and Jemima preparing to enter the sea in her stead.

"It was Esther as told us," said Rebecca. "We think we must try."

"Then I hope you will enjoy it," said Elizabeth. She gave her some money and said: "This is exactly the double of Mrs Tegg's usual charge. We will pay it to her every day. And you must say to her—that it is our way of giving her our thanks."

The day passed very slowly indeed. At midday Mrs Sibford herself brought in a nuncheon for them, saying as she left: "I see Mrs Tegg come up. She and Mrs Wicken be sisters—mother was a witch. Colonel in very good hands, you'll see. Soon be well again."

Elizabeth was very heartened by this news. Rather to their surprise, she and Mrs Wentworth consumed everything on the tray, and Elizabeth was happy to be able to decide that the lemonade was even better than Miss Bingley's. It raised her spirits a little.

The first great test of the day came at four o'clock, when the doctor's saline draught arrived. They had to decide to wake their patient in order to take it.

"I suppose we must sit him up," said Elizabeth.

"I must suppose so, too," said Mrs Wentworth.

He was almost immovably heavy.

"That must be a good sign," said Elizabeth. "*Not* wasting away."

The lavender vinaigrette took a little time to do its work; but then, quite suddenly, the Colonel sat up himself and said: "Died in the hunting field, did she? That blackguard Stornaway plotted that?"

"Try to drink this, Colonel, if you please," said Elizabeth, in her most soothing tones.

"If you tell me what it is."

"It is a saline draught, sent by the doctor."

"By the doctor, you say? Am I unwell?"

"You are in somewhat of a fever, my dear friend. Enough to cause us a little alarm."

"Then I have no wish to alarm you, Madam. You look like Mrs Collins's pretty friend. Better take Darcy if he offers. Never known him in love before."

He drank down the saline draught.

"Disgusting," he said, but without a grimace. He turned to Mrs Wentworth.

"To oblige you, Madam, anything. You have the most beautiful eyes."

Then he lay back and was asleep in ten seconds.

They exchanged a smile, principally one of relief; but the second great test was still to come.

At six o'clock John returned with the first of Mrs Wicken's potions. James was to remain overnight as some of the remedies were efficacious only if made when the sun was rising. The syrup of seaweed was in fact a jelly, to be administered with a spoon; and they were both of the opinion that the Colonel should be given clean sheets *and* a clean nightshirt. He had to be wakened again.

They were rescued from their dilemma by the return of Foston, unable to sleep.

"Colonel has been my life for many years, madam. I cannot stay away."

It was agreed that the Colonel should be given the jelly first and then have his nightshirt changed.

"If this young man will assist me."

Once more the lavender vinaigrette did its work. Once more the Colonel accepted his medicine from Elizabeth, saying only: "Better than before. Not unpleasant. If it comes from you it must benefit me."

The new remedy had to be taken every two hours exactly. John undertook to give any assistance that Foston might require, and the two ladies rather reluctantly took their leave.

As they got to the door, Elizabeth said: "Are we dining with you—or are you dining with us?"

After a moment Mrs Wentworth said: "I shall have to ask the Admiral. I am too confused by today's events."

"Then," said Elizabeth, "until later."

They exchanged a kiss.

XXVIII

It was later than Elizabeth thought. Patton, opening the door to her, asked, in a concerned voice, at what time she would like the dinner to be served.

"Oh," she said, "are we dining here? Then, in an hour's time, if you please. And send to the Wentworths to let them know."

It was already seven o'clock. In the nursery there was much to be learnt. Rebecca and Jemima had both enjoyed their first encounter with the sea so much that they wished to repeat it. They had all been down to the little beach with Mr Darcy; and the Admiral had joined them there.

"He makes very good castles, Mama," said Jane. "But they look like ships. And," she said, lowering her voice to a whisper, "Mrs Tegg has grown some more front teeth."

Elizabeth, gratefully, felt able to smile. The information even increased her confidence in Mrs Tegg's abilities.

"And I am sure she is the only person in England who could do so," she said. "All our dependence is on Mrs Tegg."

"Is she really a witch, Mama?"

"I am certainly beginning to hope so."

Their dinner was served and eaten in silence, one of consideration on Patton's part, of appreciation on theirs; and even after that it was a sombre, subdued evening. Elizabeth was only too thankful that their conversation did not stray beyond the commonplace.

She had arranged to meet Mrs Wentworth at eleven o'clock the next morning, at the lower house. There they were received by a smiling Foston, almost in a state of jubilation.

"I have to say, madam, that I believe the danger to be past. And, if you cannot believe this, I also have to say that I cannot believe it either. But it was the potion, madam, the potion that James brought very soon after sunrise."

The Colonel was found, once more, to be in a deep sleep, but of a different kind. He was breathing regularly, breathing peacefully, and with no beads of sweat on his forehead.

"Your young men, madam, if I may say so, are of the first quality, and I believe you may safely leave the nursing to me and to them. The Colonel is a large man and a heavy one, as I think you may have discovered. I cannot raise him alone."

"Then James and John are quite at your service," said Elizabeth. "It will be something new in their lives. But now you must tell me about the potion."

They moved into the dressing-room where there were some chairs.

"You must sit down," said Mrs Wentworth to Foston. "I am sure you are quite worn out."

"I am, madam, but now alive again. The potion came in an earthenware bottle with the instruction that it should be taken at once—and standing up, if possible with the sun upon the patient. It took the three of us to move him into the sunlight—as he seemed very weak at the knees—but when he understood what we were at, Colonel was very helpful. More used to giving orders than receiving them. So we stood him up and he drank it down. Then he said, 'Well, either I am dead or I am cured for ever' and asked for the pan."

Elizabeth and Mrs Wentworth remained silent, quite rooted to their chairs.

"I will not distress you, madam, with what happened next but I believe it all to have been of benefit. We got him back into bed and he said, as he fell asleep, 'I think they have done it for me'. And he looked already quite different."

"Wonderful Mrs Wicken," said Elizabeth, "and Mrs Tegg. How can we ever reward them? But what are the nursing arrangements today?"

"James is with me, madam, as you see. I have sent John off to sleep. With your permission, they will take it in turns. We must change the linen every day but the lady in the top house is very understanding."

"And you—Foston, I think?" said Mrs Wentworth. "What about you?"

"I am on guard, madam," said Foston simply. "Colonel saved my life once, in a manner of speaking. Now is the chance to return the favour."

"Then we will leave you on guard," said Elizabeth, as she got up. "The Colonel is in excellent hands. You must ask for whatever you need, perhaps from Mrs Sibford as she will know about any local delicacies. We shall not interrupt you but will call from time to time to receive the latest news."

They went up to the top house together, received once more by Patton.

"The news is even beyond the excellent," said Elizabeth to him. "I think we are both quite thirsty."

They were surprised, and pleased, to find that Mr Darcy and the Admiral had taken the children, with Rebecca and Jemima, for a picnic on the Cobb, so that they could be in position as soon as the tide left the little beach dry.

"I understand from my daughter," said Elizabeth, "that the Admiral makes outstanding castles—although they really look more like ships."

"I am delighted to hear it," said Mrs Wentworth, smiling. "I have never known him at peace with the world to such a degree. The great change from sailor to landsman is not yet quite complete, but at Lyme there is a touch of both worlds. I sometimes fear that my own daughters have too much of the Elliot to be amused by making sand castles on a beach."

The lemonade came. A simple nuncheon was served to them, alone, in the sitting-room, and they then set off, together, to join the picnic on the Cobb. As they reached the bottom of the hill, Miss Crawford came to meet them.

"News travels," she said at once, "but slowly, to Mr Pyne's house. I am indebted to my flower-seller for the latest news."

"I hope," said Elizabeth, "that the latest news is as excellent as the latest news truly is. It is the opinion of the admirable Foston that the Colonel is out of danger—but I was reluctant to involve you until I was quite certain."

"Ah, forgive me if my voice was a little sharp. I think I cannot, yet, be of any help and can only commend what is already done. But I must hope that you will wish to involve me—later."

"That, without doubt," said Elizabeth. "We were all taken so entirely by surprise that wider considerations fell by the wayside. I think I am not too much of an optimist when I say that he will be receiving visitors in a very few days' time."

"Tell me about the admirable Foston."

"Only that he feels he owes his life to the Colonel and now undertakes to nurse him entirely, with the help of James and John, our footmen. Listening between the words, I think that men may sometimes respond better to each other at that time. But when, my dear Mary, he is able to sit up, to be cosseted, to be read to, to be sympathised with—then you may be certain to be included in those duties."

"Duties I will not say," said Miss Crawford. "I think I would be of little use as a nurse."

"Elizabeth is perfectly right," said Mrs Wentworth, "to think that nurses come in *after* the surgeons have done their work. Happily there are no surgeons in this case—and *our* first duty is to enjoy our walk upon the Cobb."

It was three days before Foston came to request the presence of one of the ladies in the afternoon. Elizabeth decided to go herself and was silently amazed to find the Colonel propped up in bed, his colour excellent and his spirits high.

"I feel only," he said, "that my legs belong to someone else."

Elizabeth was slightly at a loss to know how to begin the conversation, but the Colonel forestalled her.

"I am very glad to be alone with you," he said, "to congratulate you upon your husband. It was some years, I must confess, before I was able to connect my cousin Darcy's new wife with the beautiful friend of Mrs Collins at Rosings. From the somewhat desolate shores of Halifax, Nova Scotia, I could only envy his happiness while deploring the lack of my own. And clearly such happiness is a great preservative. He looks hardly any older than he did those years ago—quite ten years younger than myself, though the difference is only six months."

"But you have been so ill. You must be a little patient. I am sure that Lyme will start your great recovery."

"I know, of course, that my redoubtable aunt Catherine has gone. I recall her being considerably impolite to you, but neither Darcy nor I was man enough to take your part. Do you have any correspondence with our cousin Anne? How do things stand at Rosings?"

"Our cousin Anne is now mistress in her own house. She lives there very comfortably with four adopted daughters."

"Four adopted daughters! Where did she find them, I wonder?"

"They are the children of that friend—Charlotte Collins. She died just over a year ago and their father is gone as missionary to Madras. It seems the arrangement makes everyone quite happy and one can only rejoice that their education is in her hands rather than in his."

"He was, as I remember, a man of more than usual solemnity. One can only have pity for the Indians."

"An under-statement, Colonel," said Elizabeth, in her pleasantest voice. "If you will allow me to say so."

"I will indeed," said he, with a dawning smile. "But now you must tell me how it was that I found Mary Crawford visiting your house."

Elizabeth did so as concisely as she could, restricting her recital only to the years of their acquaintance. Try as she would to soften her account of the recent events in Miss Crawford's life, she could not but echo in her heart some of the Colonel's more robust exclamations.

"So that brother of hers is gone, too," he said, when she had finished. "I did not know their parents, but Admiral Crawford and his wife were well-known to me, he a monster, she a saint. Apart from Mrs Grant, then, she is quite alone."

Elizabeth judged it wisest to say nothing. After a small silence the Colonel went on: "I see little change in her also. Though, if I am to be honest with myself, I was so engrossed with her friend Flora that I paid very little attention to her."

"Was she very beautiful, her friend Flora?"

"Yes," he said, rather hesitantly, "she was. I have rarely seen anyone to equal her, but that I now regard as a fault rather than a thing to boast of. No one, however, could have deserved such an end."

"No," said Elizabeth, "no one could. But perhaps this is the moment to tell you that your cousin Anne always hoped that you would bring back from Bermuda a vulgar Creole lady of enormous wealth, with a passion for purple satin and diamonds."

For the first time, the Colonel laughed.

"If that is the case, she must have altered beyond recognition. I remember her only as completely silent. But she is a little confused. Vulgar Creole ladies of that stamp occur perhaps in the Bahamas rather than in the Bermudas—*our* society was almost painfully genteel. I should have had to travel at least to Jamaica to find a lady of that kind."

Elizabeth left soon afterwards, happy to feel that the Colonel was himself once more; but she was still a little perplexed to decide when she would be able to take Mary Crawford to see him.

XXIX

It was much sooner than she expected. The next afternoon, Foston came to say that the Colonel would no longer stay in bed and that he was at his wits' end to know what to do next.

"I will come back with you," said Mr Darcy. "It is entirely too early to think of him bathing in the sea, but perhaps the warm bath might be acceptable—if, as I am reliably informed, his legs continue to belong to someone else."

To Elizabeth's great relief, Mr Darcy now took charge of the Colonel's recovery. On that first day, he went into the warm bath. On the next Gentlemen's Day, he went into the sea. His improvement was so rapid, his spirits invariably so high, that Elizabeth sometimes had difficulty in believing the evidence of her eyes.

But it was a subject which no one discussed, the lookers-on content to be bystanders and to wish a complete revival of his strength to the reluctant sufferer. There was therefore no opposition of any kind when Miss Crawford asked him to dine, with the Darcys and the Wentworths.

He condescended to be carried in a sedan-chair, "so long as no one else can see me," and Elizabeth and Mrs Wentworth followed suit. The actual entrance to Mr Pyne's house proved so narrow that it had to be accomplished one by one, the first one leaving before the second arrived. Mr Darcy bought all that remained of the flower-seller's wares and thanked her for her smiling "God Bless You".

They made a very animated party, too crowded for any formality, their proximity to one another so close, indeed, that conversation could only be general. Elizabeth found herself sharing a dressing-stool with Miss Crawford at one end of the table, while the Colonel, on account of his still stiff knee, sat at the other, actually in the doorway. The dishes were handed round, one to the other, and returned to the maidservant, who stood behind the Colonel.

Elizabeth had some difficulty in not catching Mrs Wentworth's eye when some buttered lobster made its circuit, but was able to smile when Miss Crawford said to her, in a very low voice: "Never let is be said that Miss Crawford cannot take a hint. We are adopting your diet, but for quite another reason."

She paused for a moment and then said, with her most beguiling smile: "Greed, you know, good, old-fashioned greed. There is something curiously satisfying in giving in to greed. It makes the tradesmen so happy, too, that it cannot be considered sinful."

As they left, the Colonel took Miss Crawford's hand and kissed it.

"For old times' sake," he solemnly said.

She swept him an ironical curtsey.

"Yes," she said. "For old times' sake."

There was a moon to light them home. The air was very still, prompting the Colonel to remark, as he entered his sedan-chair: "There were times in Bermuda when one imagined oneself to be in Heaven. I had not thought that air in England could be so soft, and warm—and scented," he added, with a smile. "Is it the fish, do you think, or just the seaweed? By any standards, Lyme is quite unique."

"It is neither," said Elizabeth. "It is the good wishes of all the inhabitants of this charming town. They expect you, as we expect you, to grow a little better, and a little younger, every day."

And, although she had spoken flippantly, the years did indeed seem to drop away from the Colonel. On the next day he went straight from the sea into the warm bath. In the afternoon, he accompanied the family on their walk to the Ware Cleeves where, rather to Elizabeth's disappointment, Miss Crawford was not to be found sketching. The Thursday was passed in a similar way, except that the Colonel spent the whole morning in the warm bath.

On the Friday, however, there was a change. The three of them were gathered in the sitting-room, awaiting a summons to nuncheon.

"You must look to your defences, Colonel," said Mr Darcy dryly, as he gazed out of the window. "We are surprised. Here are Elliot and Miss Bingley, looking, I think I may say, extremely pleased with themselves. We can guess what they are come to tell us."

They had not long to wait. The door opened and Patton announced them, adding in an aside to Elizabeth: "I will inform Mrs Maltby, madam."

"We are just come from the Wentworths," said Miss Bingley, "so I will not pretend that you are the first to know. But Mr Elliot has done me the honour to request my hand in marriage."

"And Miss Bingley has done me the honour to accept," said Mr Elliot.

"Then let me congratulate you both," said Mr Darcy immediately. "I feel no doubt of your happiness together. And you will allow me to present my cousin, Colonel Fitzwilliam, to you."

Bows, a courtesy, passed; Colonel Fitzwilliam murmured that he was very happy.

"And I must give you my congratulations, too," said Elizabeth. Then, more particularly to Miss Bingley: "And those of my sister Jane, though I am sure she has no inkling of the pleasure in store for her. Indeed, to my shame, I have not written to her since I came to Lyme; but now I must delay no longer."

Wine was sent for and a health was drunk.

"Have you thought of where you will live?" asked Elizabeth of Miss Bingley a little while later. "Do you mean to spend your lives entirely in London? And, what perhaps is more important—when do you mean the ceremony to take place?"

"As soon as it may be contrived," said Miss Bingley positively. "I hope I may be married from my brother's house."

Elizabeth was stricken quite to silence by this aspect of the situation, which she had not previously considered, and could, for the moment, say nothing; but she was very soon rescued by Mr Darcy.

"That would require a special licence," said he, "since you are neither of you resident in Nottinghamshire. And if you must have a special licence, what is to prevent you being married before you leave Lyme? You have only to go to Exeter and treat with the Bishop. With four horses you may do it very conveniently in a day."

Miss Bingley appeared to be fighting with herself.

"I can see all the advantages of such a plan," she said, after a small hesitation, "but it is not quite what I had hoped for."

"You would like a full romantic wedding," said Mr Darcy, with a smile, "but let me try to persuade you. Here I am sure the Admiral will support Mr Elliot. I will give the bride away, if she will permit it, and Elizabeth and Mrs Wentworth will attend her to church. You may then give the six of us a great feast at Monmouth House and the whole episode will be over in a moment."

"My love," said Elizabeth, quickly, "you speak too much as a man. I do not believe that any woman would consent to such a scheme, were an alternative to offer."

"Then what is the alternative?" asked Mr Darcy, but in his kindest voice. "There is only one that I can see. Caroline no longer has a London residence, though she could be married from our house if we were there to open it. She can go to her brother and your sister, but all these plans must still require the special licence, more especially the latter. I submit my original notion—and rest my case."

"But you quite persecute Miss Bingley," said Elizabeth, with a conviction which surprised her. "She, I am sure, wishes to be given in marriage by her brother and with his children in attendance. And a very pretty ceremony that would make."

"It is a charming picture, indeed," said Mr Elliot, "but I begin to perceive the convenience of Mr Darcy's scheme. I have no acquaintance in Nottinghamshire—in fact, I think I have never been there in my life. It is somewhere *northward*, I believe?"

Elizabeth was a little ashamed to find how pleased she was that Mr Elliot clearly considered Nottinghamshire to be quite off the map, as Mrs Tilney had done. Derbyshire, she could not but reflect, though no further northward, he must regard as equally remote. But it was at that moment that she remembered Catherine's secret hope that Mr Elliot should already have a wife and several children in Lyme.

"I am sure," she said, with a smile to Miss Bingley, "that Mr Elliot would like to be married in Lyme, as he has been for so long connected with the place. But I am adamant that the final decision should be yours."

"I *have* been long connected with this place," said Mr Elliot, the slightest of slight edges in his voice, "but my late wife's family is now dispersed. As indeed," with a glance at Miss Bingley, "I have been at some pains to make plain."

"In which you have most perfectly succeeded," said Miss Bingley pleasantly. "But I think there is another consideration here. We have the intention," she said rather more loudly, and with a satisfied look around the company, "to combine our skills and judgment in the compilation of a book to be called *A Simple Guide to Elegant Conduct*."

"We are still in dispute about the title," said Mr Elliot. "I am not sure that I do not prefer *A Certain Guide to Good Conduct*, but in either case it is a work of which our society stands in crying need. It cannot be written too soon. Perhaps," with a kind smile towards Miss Bingley, "this argues in favour of a very quiet marriage at Lyme."

"But," said Elizabeth, into the total silence that this information had produced, "who will be your authority? Have you some acquaintance at Court?"

"I think," said Mr Elliot, unable to keep the patronage out of his voice, "that we may safely consult our own manners."

"The basis of *all* good manners," said Mr Darcy, in an authoritative voice, which Elizabeth had not heard since they came to Lyme, "is consideration for the other person. With that behind them, even the most rigid requirements of *etiquette* become endurable. Without it, they shrink into mere regulation.

If you will make that the first sentence of your book, and reiterate it frequently throughout it, you may depend upon me to order a copy."

Miss Bingley had the grace to look as though such a thought had never entered her head. Even Mr Elliot's habitual complacency appeared a little punctured; but he said, with the perfect confidence which characterised his every utterance: "That is advice for those whose manners are already excellent. We must aim our arrows a little lower, since our targets are to be those who have arrived in society on the back of some newly-acquired wealth. It is for *them* to imitate *us*, in observances of one kind or another that have grown up over the years. But, in order that they may be able to do so, those observances must be made plain. And that is what I—what we—propose to do."

"Bravely spoken," said Mr Darcy, smiling now. "I do not envy you your task."

"So do we agree," asked Elizabeth, hoping she was not picking her pears before they were ripe, "that a quiet wedding here, which I think we should all enjoy, is to take place some time next week?"

"Yes," said Miss Bingley, in sudden decision. "I am sure I should be most happy to spend September in the country—and with my brother and your sister—" nodding gracefully to Elizabeth, "but I think I should be even happier to spend it in London, with my husband."

As there could be no improving on this sentiment, the discussion came to an end; and Miss Bingley and Mr Elliot very soon departed. When they were safely out of the door, Colonel Fitzwilliam, who had not otherwise spoken a word, said to Mr Darcy: "You must explain to me the attractions of Miss Bingley. Her charms appear to be only too adequately concealed."

Mr Darcy laughed, and Elizabeth with him.

"Her charms," he said, "in this instance, must lie in the possession of a profound knowledge of all formal manners, a handsome portion and, I must concede, a sense of fashion rarely to be quarrelled with. All of which she will certainly need in the role that Mr Elliot has chosen for her. She has been for some time an irritation in the family and I am especially happy to think that, once this desirable match has taken place, we may never again have to see either of them, except on the most *crowded* occasions."

"I collect, then, that this desirable match has your blessing?" said the Colonel.

"It has," said Mr Darcy. "I pray only that nothing will occur to prevent it."

XXX

On Monday it was known that Mr Elliot had gone to Exeter, with four horses. On Tuesday a note from Miss Bingley requested their presence at her wedding on Wednesday "and afterwards at Monmouth House"; and on that day the ceremony took place exactly as Mr Darcy had suggested. No just cause or impediment appeared, no living wife came storming up the aisle, and after it they progressed in stately fashion down the road to Monmouth House.

Not until the three ladies retired, after an elaborate and extensive wedding breakfast, did Elizabeth have a chance to be alone with the new Mrs Elliot. Mrs Wentworth providentially went upstairs first and Elizabeth directly said: "What did your attorney have to say? And what did Mr Elliot think about your sending for him?"

"He was impressed by my foresight," said Mrs Elliot, very calmly. "But I need not have been concerned. I find that he has very extensive property just outside Bristol. He can have no interest in my fortune at all. Compared to his, indeed, it is quite paltry. I am to have all my own money to spend on my clothes."

"Then you have set my mind completely at rest and I must wish you very happy."

Suddenly, Mrs Elliot seemed to unbend.

"Wish me good luck, Elizabeth," she said. "I hope I may have done right. I will admit to envying you your life and your husband, ever since you married him. But I will put that now behind me. Only, I think, I shall take his manners as my pattern, rather than my husband's."

She came over and kissed Elizabeth on the cheek; and Elizabeth, too astonished to say anything, quietly submitted.

They walked very slowly home, through the heat of a particularly sultry afternoon, with the Wentworths.

"It is quite strange," remarked the Admiral, "to be leaving a bridal couple *behind* in their house. Usually one is waving them away. But I understand from the passionate bridegroom that they remain in Monmouth House until the 31st, when it must be given up anyway. I believe," he went on, addressing himself to his wife, "that your cousin has acquired a wife quite as hard-headed and saving as he is himself."

"I believe he has," replied Mrs Wentworth. "I only hope that, in their efforts to out-economise each other, they do not starve themselves to death."

They parted at the Wentworths' door. It was their turn to dine with the Darcys.

The house was empty. Colonel Fitzwilliam had called every day on Mrs Grant and Miss Crawford. He had disappeared on the two previous afternoons, his limp rapidly disappearing. Today, however, Mrs Grant and Miss Crawford had taken him by carriage, with Jemima and the Darcy children, to the Great Glade in Pinhay Woods. They had gone on to visit Mrs Wicken, to thank her and to show her the results of her potions.

They did not come back until five o'clock and it was not until several minutes later, the nursery party having been despatched quite happily upstairs, that Elizabeth had leisure to examine the Colonel. He was sitting very upright in a chair by the window, but was facing into the room. He looked younger, as indeed he had been doing by the day, more alert and more at ease with himself.

"Yes?" she said to him.

He laughed before replying: "There is no concealing anything from you, my dear Elizabeth—but why should I wish to? Yes. I have Mary's promise—and she has mine."

Elizabeth gave him her hand and he kissed her cheek. Mr Darcy came over and shook his hand.

"This is the best news we have had for a long time," he said. "It casts the other doings of this day quite into oblivion."

He rang and asked for wine, the ever-competent Patton informing him that there was champagne in the cold cellar.

When this came in, there was also a letter for Colonel Fitzwilliam.

"James brought it from the Receiving Office this morning, sir," said Patton. "But you had already left."

"I am not at all sure that I want a letter," said Colonel Fitzwilliam.

They drank health and good fortune to him and Miss Crawford. Then he said: "No doubt the letter is simply to inform me that my detested sister-in-law has at last given birth to a son—which indeed I hope she has, as I find I do not particularly wish ever to go to Belford again."

Looking at it more closely, he said: "Sent to my Regimental Headquarters—and then to my Club—and now here. And—yes, it is from the family lawyer at Hexham."

Opening it, he looked at it carefully and then said: "I cannot read his lawyer's scrawl—that is more in your line than mine. Would you read it to me, Fitzwilliam? It cannot be anything private."

Mr Darcy took the letter and went right over to the window.

"'Honoured Sir,'" he read aloud, "'It is my much-lamented duty to inform you, with the deepest sympathy, that your excellent Brother, Lionel Edward, 8th Earl Belford, met with a fatal accident on the 24th ultimo.' This letter," remarked Mr Darcy, "is dated the 2nd of August. It has been nearly three weeks in the post. 'Four days after this unfortunate occurrence his widow the Countess was safely delivered of a fifth daughter and the well-being of both is now established. From this you will understand that the titles and dignities of the Earldom of Belford descend without let or hindrance upon yourself; and it is my earnest wish, and that of all connected with you, that you should present yourself in person here to take up the aforesaid titles and dignities and all that attaches to them. I am, Sir, Your Lordship's most humble servant'—some signature that I cannot read. But there is a most interesting Postscript," added Mr Darcy. "'I did not subscribe your Lordship's title on the outside of this communication lest there should be some doubt as to the recipient.'"

A complete silence fell after these words died away in the room. Colonel Fitzwilliam put his head in his hands and groaned heavily.

"May God preserve me indeed," was all he said.

Mr Darcy filled his glass again.

XXXI

Elizabeth now exchanged a glance with Mr Darcy but they remained silent. There seemed nothing to say. At last, however, Colonel Fitzwilliam sat up, emptied his glass at a draught and smiled ruefully.

"There is no escape," he said. "I hope I am man enough to accept that."

"Will it be such a punishment to you?" asked Elizabeth, gently. "Are the bad memories so deeply etched?"

"Yes," he said, "on both counts."

He held out his glass to Mr Darcy who, once more, filled it to the brim. He took a large mouthful and then put it down.

"I favour my mother's side of the family," he said. "She was, I can say without vanity, an extremely beautiful and talented woman. What she must have endured at the hands of my father I do not like to say, but the situation between my brother and myself is quite simply rooted there. He was the elder by fourteen months. As we grew up I equalled, or excelled, him in almost every field. Things which came easily to me defeated him, both in the schoolroom and out of it. It was clear, by the time I was thirteen, that I would be the taller of the two, better-looking in every way and, I can say without much doubt, more intelligent and with more social grace."

He smiled at Elizabeth.

"Which is merely to say, with more than none at all. We did not, of course, go into society at that age but my mother encouraged us in conversation when at home alone; and my brother could never find anything to say. But, when I was fifteen, my mother died, of a fever not unlike the one I have at present. I was left isolated in the family. My father could not bear to see me, because I reminded him of her, and my brother's jealousy developed into an obsession of almost homicidal proportions. The three years following my mother's death are some that I cannot bear to think of."

So saying, he got up and took a few paces through the room, an expression on his face of such distress that Elizabeth was tempted to go to him. He soon sat down again, however, where he had been before, and continued, in a dry, still voice: "I left there at eighteen and went into the Army. An excellent commission was purchased for me and I found, three years later, that my mother's fortune had been settled on me. It was not large but it must have straitened them in many ways, and it was enough to support the *appearance* of an Earl's younger son. One should remember that we were still at war. I saw some service both in Portugal and Spain."

He seemed now to be addressing himself solely to Elizabeth, so she smiled at him and said softly: "Pray continue. You must tell us all—you have our whole attention."

"You are right," he said in reply. "I could not have two more sympathetic hearers."

He refreshed himself again and then continued, speaking at a canter rather than a trot: "No doubt they both hoped the French would dispose of me for ever, but it seems I bear a charmed life. My brother had married as soon as he could, the daughter of an ironmaster at Wolverhampton with a hundred thousand pounds. Her name was Martha Weldon and she was eight years older than he. They began breeding at once—their eldest daughter must be nearly twelve. Luck, however, was not on my side, as I did not want the title; and neither was it on his, as he did not want me to have it either. Our letter does not tell us the nature of his fatal accident, but one may be quite certain that it was something so foolish that we shall never be informed."

"I believe," said Mr Darcy, "that the Wentworths are arriving—it being our turn to give them dinner," he said, in explanation to the Colonel. "What would you have us do— or say?"

"Nothing," was the immediate reply. "Say nothing of this to them, but by all means apprise them of my engagement. *That,*

I think, can only give them pleasure, while I reserve my other feelings until I can make some sense of them. But—no," he said, in rather a hurried voice, "I change my mind. Say nothing of either event, I think. I must go to Mary in the morning and release her from this engagement if she wishes. We spent the afternoon discussing where we would live and it certainly was not to be at Belford."

"If that is how you feel," said Elizabeth, "you will find yourself completely mistaken in Miss Crawford."

"I can only regard what has befallen me as utter disaster."

"In which case," said Mr Darcy, smiling at him, "you could not do better than have Miss Crawford at your side."

It was a tantalising evening. Elizabeth, bursting with knowledge which she very much wished to share with Mrs Wentworth, was obliged to restrict her conversation to other topics. Fortunately Miss Bingley's wedding—which seemed as if it had taken place several weeks before—provided ample material; and the gentlemen conducted a discussion on the state of things in France—which appeared to Elizabeth to be one of more than total confusion—which kept them happily occupied until the tea and coffee had been drunk.

The next morning the Colonel—or the Earl, as Elizabeth now tried to think of him—breakfasted, as usual, alone. It was Elizabeth's day for sea-bathing and she returned to the house at the same time as Mr Darcy came back from his ride. They were seated together, some time later, when the Colonel returned with Miss Crawford.

"I can see," said Mr Darcy to her, with one of his happiest smiles, "that you do not mean to overturn your engagement."

"Indeed I do not," returned Miss Crawford at once, "and I do not think that any other man in the kingdom would have thought of it. I begin to fear, in fact, that I may have heavy work persuading him to be an Earl—and I have begun by obliging him to send for the family conveyance so that we may travel under the benefit of our own arms. I only hope it may not be a coach dating from the time of Charles the Second—I receive the *strangest* picture of this northern country. My dear

Henry is of opinion that, if there is a carriage at all, it will have been purchased by the present Countess who will wish to appropriate it for her own use only. But I do not at all regard that as a reason for not demanding it."

Elizabeth laughingly agreed with her. The Earl, as she was now determined to think of him, already looked quite different. She was happy to note that the gloom which had enveloped him the night before had been dissipated completely. He now looked across at Miss Crawford and smiled, but it was Mr Darcy who said: "You would be much better advised to ask them to meet you at some convenient hostelry in Durham or Newcastle, I think. If the conveyance should be of the mediaeval kind, you will not want to travel in it any further than you must. And you will be able to get as far as that, you know, in relative comfort."

"Darcy is right, my love," said the ninth Earl Belford. "It is only necessary to *arrive* flying our own colours. Indeed I think his an excellent scheme and will certainly act upon it."

"And dressed entirely in the deepest mourning," added Miss Crawford. "He for someone he detested or, at least, for someone who detested him, and I for someone I have never met. I hope, at least, that they will not wait for us to attend his funeral."

"Recollect, my dearest Mary, that this letter is now three weeks old. Even in our northern country, he would not keep so long."

"I have read too many novels," said Miss Crawford, turning to Elizabeth, "to allow the present situation to pass me by. It must be the ambition of every *romantic* heroine to be married in black. I do not believe that even Mrs Radcliffe ever thought of such a thing. And one thing that I have in great abundance," she said, though with a catch in her voice, "is a supply of black clothes."

"I had never thought of you as a romantic heroine," admitted Elizabeth. "Heroine, certainly, but of the more practical kind. In which connection I will ask you directly—where do you mean to be married?"

"But here in Lyme, without a doubt. We shall take a leaf out of Miss Bingley's book. Henry will go to Exeter in Mr Elliot's wake. How surprised the Bishop will be to have two applications in one week. If Bishop's wife there be, he will be able to give her a new bonnet."

"Will you do so?" asked Mr Darcy of the Earl. "In that case I should like to come with you. I am curious to see what is involved in the purchase of a special licence."

This mood, sometimes frivolous, sometimes arch, persisted over nuncheon. Elizabeth was only too relieved to see the Earl soften and settle. He went off with Mr Darcy after they had finished eating, and Elizabeth was taken quite by surprise when Miss Crawford asked if she would accompany her home and look closely at her wardrobe.

"I have found a seamstress already, but as you are the one of us who has been most recently in London, I would greatly appreciate your comments—and your taste. The bodice grows longer and longer. Indeed, I think I have never been asked to have a *waist* before—it is something entirely new. I hope we have only to insert a band *at* the waist to bring everything up to the mode. And now it is my turn to tell your cousin Anne that I have diamonds but no purple satin yet. After the end of full mourning perhaps."

"I will write to her myself," said Elizabeth.

They walked quietly through the afternoon heat, to find that Mrs Grant was resting. They went upstairs to Miss Crawford's room, where her maid and the seamstress were waiting.

It took longer to resolve everything to everyone's satisfaction than might have been expected. It was necessary, first of all, to decide which dresses could be submitted to this alteration and then to determine precisely how it should be done. But the decisions were made. Some eight garments were removed to the workroom, and the seamstress promised to have them ready by the following Tuesday.

"Because we mean the ceremony to take place on Wednesday," said Miss Crawford. Then, as they were by now alone, she went on: "We go first to London, I must suppose to

Grillon's or the Pulteney. It is a new experience to be a stranger in London. I must see my attorney before I disappear and—I can say this only to you—I have some thought of having my marriage consummated *before* we go to Belford. I fear that Henry's detestation of the place will put him off entirely."

Elizabeth only nodded. Then she said, in a serious voice: "There are many things to be considered, indeed. Your new responsibilities could daunt someone with less courage. But I would like to tell you, in the most complete sincerity, that I think you very well suited to each other and very well placed to overcome all the obstacles that I fear you will find in front of you. You will require some good luck, and a lot of good judgment, but I am sure that no one can doubt your happiness together."

"That," said Miss Crawford, "is exactly what I wished to hear. Thank you. I was afraid, you know, that you would think I had run mad."

"Not for one moment," said Elizabeth. "I am as attached to the Colonel as a cousin could be. I am *delighted* to feel that he has found a friend as well as a wife."

"Henry has only one drawback that I can see and I shall help him to overcome it. He is too much the younger son. Now my brother Henry was never a younger son and, although he was never an elder son either, he always behaved like one. So I have some experience of *that* species—and I certainly do not mean to be incommoded by this *other* Countess, even though her name is Martha."

"No, *indeed*," said Elizabeth.

"I said that I was pleased to know she was the daughter of an ironmaster since that must mean that there would be, at the least, a closed stove in the kitchen. One quite imagines, you know, that until recently all the cooking was done over an open fire in the Great Hall. But Henry said he would not be surprised if she took all the improvements she had made herself away with her."

"Surely that must be impossible?" said Elizabeth. "Many of them must be—what do they say?—fixtures and fittings; and she could never survive the odium, or the ridicule, of doing such a thing. Do you have any notion of where she will go? I hope there is not a Dower House."

"There is not," said Miss Crawford, in a voice of the deepest satisfaction. "The Dowagers were simply stored away in one of the northern towers, where I understood they lived *for ever*. I hope we may persuade her to buy a villa in the Regent's Park. If she has five ugly daughters to dispose of she will need every penny of her hundred thousand pounds, which Henry says must be returned to her. Unless of course those daughters favour their paternal uncle, or their grandmother I should rather say, in which case they acquire an aunt who will love them all inordinately."

"I understood from Mr Elliot that she is extremely plain and very sour."

"So Henry informs me, though how he knows must be a puzzle, since he has never met her himself."

"I had certainly not understood that."

"I believe it was indicated, quite from the beginning, that Henry was not welcome there after his brother's marriage— which would be her doing, I suppose. She must be tearing her hair and rending her garments. But if she wants a battle," she went on, after a moment, "I am *perfectly* happy to give her one."

Miss Crawford stayed to make some change in her dress, so Elizabeth went downstairs alone, to find Mrs Grant in her sitting-room, presiding over a tea-table.

"I know what you have been doing," she said, as Elizabeth came in. "Dressmaking, or anything to do with it, makes one very thirsty."

She looked so calm and satisfied, so quietly triumphant in-deed, that Elizabeth found the courage to say: "Congratulations being in order, Mrs Grant, I have it in my heart to wonder if some commiseration might not be offered to you? Mary has been your companion now for some time, and Northumberland is a long way off."

"Yes," said Mrs Grant, "we have lived very comfortably together and I shall miss her, I am sure, every day of my life.

But no one could cavil at the match she is making, or the interesting and, one might say, demanding life she is to embrace. I have no doubt at all that she will do it very well and the husband she has chosen, from the little I have seen of him, appears to be a man with everything to recommend him."

"Have you decided what you will do yourself?"

"I have. This merely confirms a decision I had come to already. My one reservation to settling in Lyme was the inevitability, as it seemed, of Mary's dying an old maid. Now that this has happily been avoided, I mean to build myself a villa here—large enough to contain her family and, I would hope, yours—whenever they choose to come for a long visit. I have found good health here, at last, and do not ever mean to leave it."

"That is an invitation," said Elizabeth, with her warmest smile, "that we should all accept with the greatest pleasure."

XXXII

The time now seemed to pass most unacceptably quickly. Between her regular activities, her bathes in the sea and walks on the Cobb and to the Ware Cleeves, and her new position as mentor to Miss Crawford in all the concerns of her wardrobe, Elizabeth never seemed to have a moment to spare. A milliner in the town was re-trimming Miss Crawford's mourning bonnets and these, with the altered dresses, were all brought home on Tuesday.

Mr Darcy and the Earl had travelled to Exeter on the day before, so it was on the Wednesday morning, exactly one week after Miss Bingley's wedding, that Elizabeth found herself awaiting the arrival of Miss Crawford at the church. She was to come, with Mrs Grant, in the carriage in which the bride and bridegroom were later to travel.

They were all soberly dressed, though no actual mourning had been found for the bridegroom. This he was to acquire in London. He had already gone into the church, with Mr Darcy and Mrs Wentworth, leaving Elizabeth with the Admiral, who was to give the bride away.

"Only seldom," said he to Elizabeth, "does one participate at a wedding without any reservations, with perfect calm and confidence indeed. I hope with all my heart they will be happy."

Miss Crawford did not keep them waiting. She arrived precisely at eleven o'clock on the Admiral's watch, a sombre and elegant figure in black silk, with a large veiled bonnet. She carried no flowers.

"Bless my soul," said the Admiral. "I had not thought. But they leave at once, of course. A bride in black, indeed, makes it an occasion."

Elizabeth and Mrs Grant followed them into the church, where she was amused to find her own children and nearly all her own servants, the Earl's valet and Miss Crawford's maid, the flower-seller and Mr and Mrs Elliot. Quite how they had all been informed of the occasion Elizabeth could not think, until she remembered that Lyme was a very small place.

The ceremony over, the register signed, the bridal couple came down the aisle looking so perfectly happy that everyone who saw them started to smile. Their appearance at the door of the church was the signal for a magnificent peal of bells, arranged without their knowledge by the parson. They continued for some time, and so loudly, that all conversation became impossible.

As she kissed her before climbing into the carriage, the new Countess said to Elizabeth, in her ear: "I depend on your correspondence, dearest Elizabeth. But you must allow me to write to you first."

"I already await your letter," replied Elizabeth, at the top of her voice, "and with the greatest impatience. Pray make it a *very* long one!"

They drove away. The small group left behind hesitated for a moment as to whether to go down the steps into the Church Road or out of the gate into Monmouth Street.

They were rescued from this dilemma by Mrs Elliot, who indicated, by an elaborate series of signs, so clamorous and intrusive were the bells, that she would be glad to see them once more at Monmouth House; and they set off in her wake.

Their visit was by way of a leave-taking and did not last very long. After the customary cakes and lemonade Mrs Grant, in whose house the wedding breakfast was to be held, began to depart. Elizabeth had the presence of mind to ask Mrs Elliot if she should write to the Bingleys, apprising them of her marriage; and after a very short consideration, Mrs Elliot said that she would prefer to do so herself.

Mr Darcy was asked by Mr Elliot why the bride had been in black and such was his lucid and comprehensive answer that no room was left for any discussion. The two men very civilly agreed to inform each other whenever they should be in London and the party then broke up. Elizabeth found herself feeling that she was escaping from something, leaving Monmouth House for the last time.

Mrs Grant accompanied them, to her own enormous satisfaction, on foot and the breakfast took place in a mood of quiet elation, the five participants having no criticism of the ceremony or doubts about the future of the marriage they had witnessed. Mrs Grant in fact echoed the Admiral, when she said she had never before assisted at a wedding about which she had no reservations.

It was not until she was walking along the path behind the beach, on Mr Darcy's arm, that Elizabeth was struck, with inescapable force, by the knowledge that tomorrow would be her last day for bathing in the sea. A small exclamation resulted.

"And are you quite well, Elizabeth?" asked Mr Darcy, but not at all anxiously.

"Yes, perfectly," said Elizabeth at once. "But I have just assimilated the fact that we leave this charming place on Saturday."

"It has been a most memorable two months," he replied, holding her hand a little more tightly. "I have become well acquainted with my children. I have grown more in love with my wife. We have made true friends in the Wentworths. We have disposed for ever of Miss Bingley, since the Elliot parties will in future be of too elevated a nature to include us; and we have assisted my cousin Fitzwilliam, whom I have always greatly liked, to rediscover a wife who cannot do otherwise than suit him perfectly. In addition, and almost as an afterthought, we are all—ourselves, our children, nursemaids, cooks, valets, grooms and footmen—in a state of high good health never before achieved. And all this, one can barely believe, in little more than eight weeks. Truly one can say from one's heart—beautiful, wonderful Lyme."

"It does me good to hear you talk like that," said Elizabeth. "I echo your every opinion. And—perhaps—this is the moment to tell you that we expect an addition to our family. He—for I am sure he will be a he—should be born in April."

Mr Darcy did not speak, but raised her hand to his lips and kissed it.

They dined that evening at the inn, joined by Mrs Grant. They bathed as usual on Thursday and then the packing began. Elizabeth took the children for a walk to the Ware Cleeves and on the Friday they paid a final visit to Captain D'Arcy Engineer. Jane and Anne had collected some wild flowers for him as a present and these were persuaded, with some difficulty, to remain on the wall above him, at least until they were out of sight. The little beach at the Pool was wholly covered by the sea.

So it was in a slight spirit of gloom that Elizabeth set off with Mr Darcy for their last dinner with the Wentworths. Mrs Grant was also there, as were some other visitors to the inn. The fashionable season at Lyme was about to start.

The Admiral, however, had caused champagne to be served.

"Not because I rejoice at your going, I hasten to say," he said at once, "but because your presence here has so greatly enhanced our pleasure in being at Lyme. While wishing you both the best of excellent health, I would like also to express the wish—that we may meet here again next year."

They drank to each other and exchanged the calm smiles of perfect friendship.

"I had intended," said Mr Darcy, "to keep this piece of information until tomorrow, but I think the moment has arrived. I have to tell you, my dearest Elizabeth, that I have purchased all Mr Elgood's houses and that we shall indeed be able to meet here again next year."

If Mr Darcy had meant to create a small sensation, as Elizabeth certainly suspected, he succeeded to admiration. Only Mrs Grant looked as if she had been in the secret before.

"And Mrs Grant will occupy *our* house, my love, for this winter, so that she may keep her eye on the house that Mr Elgood is building for *her* a little higher up the hill. He will entirely rebuild our two smaller houses, too, enlarging them both."

"Then that," said Mrs Wentworth, "must be the best news that we could possibly expect, unless perhaps—Elizabeth?"

"I have told Mr Darcy," said Elizabeth, and then stopped.

"And I have told the Admiral," said Mrs Wentworth. "So let us drink once more—to Lyme and to our diet of lobster."

"And perhaps," said Elizabeth, struck by a sudden idea, "if all goes well with us both, Mrs Grant would do us the honour of being godmother to our babies? I wish to have an anchor in this town."

Mrs Grant indicated her assent with a little bow of her head, but was clearly too moved to be able to speak.

"I think that an excellent notion," said Mrs Wentworth. "But we must not forget Catherine's herb-woman too completely."

It was an evening of no common pleasure to them all. Their farewells were tempered with the knowledge of "next year". In bidding goodbye to the excellent landlord, they were able to say they would be back, with certainty. Mrs Grant went home in a sedan chair and they were greeted by the two men who carried her. The hill up to their house seemed shorter, and less steep, than usual.

In the morning, their exodus began early. Trunks and boxes began to be carried out of the houses at eight o'clock, though they were not to leave until eleven. They would spend the Sunday at Sherborne, as they had done on the way down.

But no sooner had Elizabeth finished her breakfast than Jane and Anne came in to see her.

"Mama," said Jane, "we wish to give Mrs Tegg a new bonnet."

"Because," said Anne, "you can smell the one she wears."

"We went to the shop yesterday with Rebecca," said Jane.

"But we had not enough money," said Anne.

"Then, my loves, I will come with you at once. I hope I have some money by me."

Mr Darcy, witness to this scene, put his hand in his pocket and emptied some coins into hers.

"Thank you," she said, and then she looked at them. "But I promise to buy only one bonnet. Here is enough for half-a-dozen."

It was a stolen excursion, back into Lyme, and doubly pleasurable as she had not expected to see it again for a year. The milliner was waiting for them, all smiles. Mrs Tegg, fortunately not too far out into the bay, was overcome and bestowed a kiss on both the little girls, which they bore with fortitude.

"It will be a boy," said Mrs Tegg. "You'll see. And the other ladies, too."

As they got back to the house, panting slightly but very pleased with themselves, Mr Darcy stood by the front door with Alexander. He gave each of his daughters a kiss.

"That was a kind and very thoughtful thing to do," he said. "I am very proud of you both."

They walked together up the hill and climbed into the carriage.

The children blew a kiss to Lyme; and their cavalcade moved off.